"A Suite Invitation"

Never Say Never

John E. Morgan

JEMORGAN
PUBLISHING

ISBN: 978-1-963851-13-7 (Paperback)
978-1-963851-14-4 (Ebook)

JE MORGAN
PUBLISHING

JE MORGAN Publishing

CONTENTS

Closure

Slender was appreciated in all its glory,
But her full-figured sister is this story;
Not to be neglected and always respected ...

I like dominoes set by pride, arrogance, and a particular kind of woman questioned the stages of my life, framed by seven deadly sins falling whose aloofness held my attention. Her persona had been present since the beginning of time. The Grecian philosopher-historian Hesiod referred to her as Pandora. She was humanity's first woman, created from clay and assigned to punish mankind because Prometheus, the immortal, stole fire from the gods and bestowed it upon mankind. Pandora's gifts from the gods included beauty and charm. However, she was also taught to be deceitful, stubborn and curious. The gods used these qualities in hiding illnesses and hardships in a box and tempted Pandora to open it. She released the maladies into the world but unintentionally left Hope trapped inside.

I defied naysayers and hypocrites who interpreted God's Laws. It had me one step from entering the gates of Hell because my alter ego Shane convinced me to pass up a dried fish filet for a pepperoni cheesesteak pizza on a meat-forbidden Friday. My venerable pastor asked me to describe this Shane, who stood tall and dark, with a slender build and a ready smile. "He looks like you," the pastor replied. There was no more to be said. I had to get away from clouded beliefs that held me in bondage. Shane and I made quite a pair, though we were one; I attributed all my missteps and arrogance to him. The years advanced, with Shane getting into trouble only he could find. Nevertheless, we appreciated the same women, particularly the one with a soft caramel complexion and Pandora-braided corn-roll extensions streaked with gold. She wore dark designer glasses and a baseball cap with a ponytail trailing the center of her back. Tight jeans and a denim jacket complemented a lush and firm body, while high-heeled open-toed sandals graced her feet.

She went by the name of Brook-Lynn and spoke in a New York Georgia buttermilk drawl that belied the fact that the farthest south she'd been was Jersey City. She wanted her freedom and explained how it would be wise to call her Brook and not expect her to become anyone's sugar mama. She was not a clinging vine, which would tie her down to one man. She used her charm cleverly when sensuous lips curled into a 'sweet invitation', hiding her past as I did mine. "We may love, just don't get attached to me," she said adding that she'd be gone by daylight. "You may want to stay awhile," I suggested. The corners of her mouth curled into a smile as she replied, "We'll just have to find out; won't we?" Her flair for adventure mirrored the wandering spirit in me. "It's all about capturing time in a bottle," I said as we began an acquaintance as pen pals on a social dating site. I was taken by a photo featuring her seated in a full-length mink, fat legs flashing and a now- familiar smile that could chase the clouds away. It was such a corny line, I thought apologetically, and wondered how Shane would have answered. Certain rules would have to apply for those of us who met on a digital social network. We had a past life that created a dilemma in the present. Shane reasoned that this pending mystery was too good to pass up, or waste years wondering what could have been. The outcome may not be lasting or fair though it may be worth the gamble. When it's time to go, she and I will do so without alibis that turn out to be lies. Friendship will die; let parting be painless or allowed to flounder in the sand. (It became a tacit agreement we lived by for nearly eight years. We tossed caution to the wind in making allowances that we would pay for later.) Our trust showed the way in the evening glow through the Hudson Valley and into the Catskills.

Shane stepped in to intercede. "Not today, my brother," I said, marking the day to discovering all about Brook: a mad roller coaster ride with seats for two, a bumpy road too late to turn back. We were never in one spot for long, exploring the five boroughs and the Long Island Sound. We sailed beneath the GW Bridge, a gateway through the Hudson, and rediscovered the cliffs and valleys of the Palisades. We rode through Connecticut and Ocean City and outraced eighteen- wheeler trailers on dark, lonely Carolina back roads. Small towns knew us as adventurers with a fetish for three-card Monte and slot machines.

"What's stopping you?" Brook asked that day at Riverside Park when we first met. She was fine, sexy with a baseball cap whose brim had me speaking to catch a glimpse of her amber eyes. I fought giving into an overwhelming impulse just to kiss her. Neither of us was talking about the past that refused to let us escape into a fantasy. Truth got smothered by wet, steamy kisses and strumming fingers across her soft belly. She held the coaxing to sleeping passion bursting from her throat. I rocked between her flailing limbs, riding into thick carpeting. We rolled onto her belly, bucked and plunged, profound and wet, across an upholstered ottoman. Sphincter spasms quaked like a knotted silk cable being drawn through me in summoning convulsions to a bittersweet cacophony of pleasure. Love flowed and then exploded in an infinite passage of inane adjectives and flashing lights.

There was another side of Brook-Lynn that I was beginning to know. She attacked like a trapped cobra if forced to go against her will. Only this time I was her priority as she became mine, and yet I couldn't help feeling that we were running against time. She appeared anxious, searching the gambling hall for a hot slot machine, but finally chose to sit next to a dreadlocked Baja, a friend of ours, rather than sit near me. Was it something I said? Or was it someone, somewhere she would rather be, other than with me? Nevertheless, the daylight hours belonged to me, though filled with intrigue. Our arguments had been either about my taking my birthday for granted or missing a country road turn-off. I became the envy of all when she walked by my side with a sex-charged body that had men bursting through red lights at busy traffic intersections. "Watch the driver," she said, flirting with him as he eyed her fat legs and tight denim skirt. The driver's girlfriend noticed her man's wandering eye. She elbowed his groin, sending their vehicle barreling into oncoming traffic. Pedestrians scampered from meeting the Grim Reaper in the aftermath of a twisted wreck.

I had no idea how dangerous Brook could be; however, Shane knew: Angel or Satan's daughter, or perhaps a little of both? Secrets lay hidden: a significant other, a scorned lover; a woman's quiet desire to be loved by another woman? Instincts urged us to proceed with caution. The lightning in a bottle I hoped to capture came at a price: losing my thoughts, my beliefs and everything I owned. Would it be worth it? Brook's always-ringing cell phone served to remind me of her past, my immediate competition and a threat to our intimacy. It showed in her eyes. Kisses became hard and abrupt. I felt a gnawing emptiness in the pit of my stomach, signaling an imminent good-bye; even so, losing her fueled the passion within me. I didn't want to appear overly eager or threatened like her past lovers who had come to me. I grappled with her minister's decree to come forward as if it would grant a stay of execution. He called all sinners to the altar. I wasn't about saving my soul; I was making a commitment starting over; I was willing to try. I forgot our tacit agreement. Shane suddenly appeared. "My brother, you were definitely the topic for discussion after your appearance at the altar. Word got back that you were merely stalking," he said, ending with how laughter and ridicule rang out about how Brook didn't look pleased.

She possessed Pandora's inbred quality that mirrored her father's skill in getting whatever he wanted from women, a most ardent talent Brook used against men in getting whatever she wanted. The predator lures the prey, smothers it and then retreats to a safe haven to enjoy it. Soon, she moves on from where she came in search of another. She becomes bored and uses God as her alibi. I remained aware of wildflowers, particularly the rose with hidden thorns. It was fascinating how she lost her contact lens when we were making love and spooning across the hood of my sedan in the shadows of the Palisades valley. "Fools rush in where strangers never go," cried a favorite serenade. Bright September and autumn's lament won't let me forget Brook-Lynn. When I moved to kiss her, she replied, "What's stopping you?" I took her against a cobbled stone wall lining the walkway leading to the deepest underbrush of Riverside Park.

History slipped to past summers, reminding how passion echoed from the basement of an old-school house. A conference table, a tattered carpet, and a swivel chair became the players. I at no time wanted to admit Brook and I met too late. What good would it have done then, when neither of us cared, nor would we have listened? I plunged to passion's calling with failing limbs curling and pummeling to tightly drawn curtains and a securely locked door.

This saga had to play out; let the cards fall where they may. Recounting gave a little closure to a friendship consummated in the shadows of Riverside. She peeled her black spandex to her broad hips and then wrenched me from my zipper. Grinding, sighing, she shifted. I surged upward and into her. Spasms rushed, exploding in cascading rivulets. From the crotch of a split oak tree, I held each limb and rose again, awakening night crawlers. The squirrels stood watch.

We played in the autumn mist and selfishly embraced the present. Denial rushed like a burst water pipe. Arrogance spun out of control. Memories had mingled beneath snow flurries at Harlem River Drive with a kiss before the final bell struck twelve on New Year's Eve. The silent railroad depot in Greenwich, Connecticut stood witness with tall city lamps casting ghostly halos in the fresh falling snow. We dined at Red Lobster. Ice crystals shone brightly along Route 58 in Nyack. A piercing blue light danced across a white gold topaz diamond in answer to unlikely possibilities.

Four years had passed since I saw her last. I cursed the traffic rerouted down the Major Deegan Expressway. There was no escape from what Brook-Lynn meant to me, and if I saw her again, it would be too soon. Her betrayal left me cold and indifferent. Everything went wrong. Self-respect lay in the debris like broken glass.

I sped down the University Avenue Exit 9 with a little thought of pulling over to call her. Congratulations were in order, proving all was well with me as I passed her door. But who was I fooling? Excuses couldn't hide what I dared not tell anyone: Discarding lovers was a game she played. We're daughters mimicking the sins of their fathers? If so, then this apple didn't fall too far from the tree. Funny, after loving I often felt the urge to drop her. However, she was in my blood. My mind stayed in overdrive. I couldn't help feeling she returned to her reality. Age reminded that chance at the brass ring had become more distant for some; the creature comfort that a home in Upper Westchester – Clarksville area may be in reach. Her best chance of a future lay with family, though it may not be the current one, perhaps another unsuspecting churchgoing, searching holy-roller whose path led to the bedroom. Still, I struggle with her persona both night and day, trying to make sense of this comedy. Perhaps she feels the time is slipping with each grain. I had to accept her future would be without me. I would not have understood had she trusted me to do so. Perhaps I wouldn't; a price one pays for being a gambler. Our dreams were buried in a rock slide along the West Highway that took us to Tryon Park and finally to Riverdale. I went through Hell and now my Purgatory waits. I couldn't deny the beauty of our relationship. It left me stranded at 161st Yankee Stadium, a quarter of a mile from the Harlem River Drive.

I rose from the confusion, disappointments, and setbacks. Memories became footsteps in the sand. I still had a long way to go to pass through a personal Inferno. The sun peeked into the sky. I picked up a trumpet and continued on stage telling my story in musical verse. It satisfied the emptiness, for the moment, and then I was alone again but found the resolve not to allow myself to become a footnote to stupidity in anyone's realm of friends, particularly Brook-Lynn's. Accusations became a comedian's trove of lopsided assumptions, disbelief, and pain. The past became a closed door, and I wanted to leave it that way. However, my demons wouldn't allow it, for now I had to pass through a lonely place where time stood still: Purgatory.

Memories continued to plague. Nevertheless, New York City wouldn't allow emotions to fester, with intimacy slipping like sand through a paper bag. Long after Brook and I exchanged rings: "It's something to remember me by," she said. I was at a loss as to what she meant then: We promised never to flaunt, or to disrespect. There was little shame in a daring tryst that had us spending our summers along a Seafront coastline, or beneath a hanging city lamp on Barrow Street in a beat-up Honda. We basked in a glowing sunset at the Christopher Street pier. I held her close; the mimes danced along the concrete boardwalk and merrily disappeared into the setting sun. We dined at an East Indian restaurant off McDougal Street where an open bay window showcased transients mingling among the Village people. Time became a floating petal to a wilting rose [flower]. I had no idea how I would I say good-bye to Brook-Lynn. I felt so low that the only place for me was up: I ascended from the depths with Shane; he never left.

I began to see that for every light that fades something beautiful remains. Memories scaled the Grand Marriott in the midst of a revolving stage featuring a panoramic view of the city stretching across the Hudson and into New Jersey. I called it a leap of Faith but Shane, preaching Harlem's wisdom, referred to it as stupidity. Brook was laughing with them, or running from me. I couldn't determine whether it was fear, hate, or shame. Perhaps all the above would apply. I gave up my pride when asking her out; her answer was no! All remained closed to speculation; the saga finished its run. I was alone; misery had me by the throat and was dragging me back into the

Inferno. I fell so far. I was no longer a priority, nor was I of any importance to me. A bullet was in the chamber, and I was ready to pull it. I was sure to give up what I owned, walk away from my home to show that I was for real —that this married man would start all over. I solved the riddle of the footprints in the sand: HE was carrying me. Trust obscured the reality for the sake of love. I had no guarantee about Brook or me other than arrogance and pride with a blind leap of Faith. "There is an old saying, my brother, about leopards not changing their spots," Shane said; repentance was an alibi for everything other than the truth. I could live with that had Brook told me she was seeing someone and left God out of it as the cause for repentance. However, even God was betrayed. Why claim God as the director of intentions when it was Eve who had always been the orchestrator?

"You're trying to turn back the clock," Shane scoffed, adding, "Brook is long gone; she chooses another path. You got to let her go." My portrait of Brook shattered, and in its place were broken glass fragments. I won't try putting it back together. Jagged edges will cut and you will bleed. Shane said, "No matter how brave we try to be, we're not always courageous but rather docile and accepting. Our crime was in being human. We have our frailties and disappointments, proving life doesn't always come in a neat package."

I renewed my faith in love and found God. He lives with the change of the four seasons, when all is pure and bursting with a new beginning. I'm blessed with passion once more; I lost it for a while. My God is stubborn; he hadn't given up on me though I denounced HIM as HE carried me, and yet I look forward to where HE will lead. It is HIS call; perhaps I'll finally discover my Lackawanna.

Until then, I travel the Palisades, longing for the silence of the cold autumn air, or just an elusive breeze teasing that last leaf to fall before winter. I write and practice my music; far from being perfect and perhaps better I remain that way because perfection gets nailed to a cross. Should anyone travel the

Palisades overlooking the Hudson, one might hear a serenade from a gushing brook with sound entwined by a silver-plated trumpet or the passionate sighs of a well-satisfied woman. You may see me wandering through long-abandoned ruins of dreams left behind, and replacing them with new ones. I've solved the riddle of the footsteps in the sand, and sometimes when the feeling hits, I live as a gambler with a fetish for three-card-Monte. Would I do it all again should Brook reappear? I needn't tell when, where, why or how; that's another story. I'll never hate her for the game she played with me. Who am I to throw stones? Let a smile or a wink suffice in keeping that answer to myself. I'll play the cards that were dealt me. How else will I find my Lackawanna? I'll always appreciate the memories: After all, they don't leave like people do. They just hang around waiting for someone or something to stir things up … Like a taste for lemon-roasted chicken.

The Procession

A toast to her, Sharing glory
With connoisseurs.
Women.

Saint James wasn't any less pious, or about to be out-sanctified by another congregation. All the people in the congregation were doing battle with their own personal demons. Conflicts hidden in quiet smiles and flowery speeches became messages with a double meaning. Sister Rachel's eyes fluttered beneath a floppy brim. The Reverend was the cause. His eyes burned like hot coals and beckoned her to him. She squirmed, wondering if he could keep a secret. She fanned herself. Beads of sweat appeared above her upper lip. The Reverend called for an "Amen!" from the congregation. Rachel moaned for 'Mercy'. She appeared dazed. Her raven locks streaked with gray curled about her ears like her lover's hot breath, sending chills down her spine when he whispered her name. The prayer bench squeaked; her thick limbs sprouted fluttering wings, smothering a buzzing vibrator nestled in the crotch of her panties. Her soft white blouse and navy blue, gold button double-breasted blazer played to her dazzling blood red burgundy skirt inching across her thighs.

Services had ended and a reception was held. Men flocked with good wishes and eyes riveted to her large, tapering limbs perched in stilettos. Gossip swirled, but Rachel remained aloof, returning home and preparing dinner for the family's gathering. Her husband had long since passed away. She missed him and now needed professional counseling to get her through this lonely period. Until then she remained lost in daydreams. One afternoon she stopped by the Reverend's chambers to confess her longing and questioning whether it was absolution she needed. She wouldn't have given the learned Baptist minister the time of day but desire had a way of making liars out of devout Christians. Disharmony flowed from the podium to the pews.

"You bastard!" Rachel whimpered. The Reverend had her against a wall and was cupping her massive rear while drawing her skirt across her thighs.

She tried pushing him away but lost all resolve, liking what he was doing to her despite it being against her will. His tongue searched her palate. He drew the breath from her lungs. Her deceased husband left her in wonder at what it would be to taste passion's bittersweet fruit. The devil in the white collar claimed her. Delirium! Aggression! Submission! Her body heaved and kicked, hooking the back of a sofa. He buried his face into the seat of her crotch. Thick limbs pounded.

"Ooh! Ooh!" He was in her. White-hot embers seared in a flash. Thick cheeks clapped. Nerves crumbled and snapped! Tears streamed. She couldn't run even if she wanted to. Panties had a stranglehold on her ankles. Rachel grabbed her panties and headed for the door. "What? Why? No more?" the Reverend cried. "Sorry," Rachel said, striking him with her soaking thongs, "your time just ran out!" She behaved, playing a game. It inflamed. He was well aware of her sweet fragrance. His eyes caressed her. He would do more if she would let him, but she smiled. The Reverend lost his mind. He leaped and buried deep. Rachel arched to dislodge, but the friction pushed her to the edge with a burning urge to piss. It was good. The Rev plunged and then lay still to prolong the sweetness she was getting and giving to him. He clenched but thrust, sending more in length and girth before spewing his seed in a sweet, orgasmic rush.

Sweet Magnolia

She stirred man's fantasies

Sweet Magnolia, from Macon Georgia, I sip the wine from your lips; you move in a slow grind, a sensual rotating twist from your hips meeting a subtle upward thrust. I lose myself in all your charms; it's only a dream that tears me apart, like a twisted dagger in the heart. And all the while I lie in wonder and ask 'why' of a union that lasted for just moments, along with frustration for letting trust become a weakness. Enough! So, I'll turn the page. However, I have been the target. So sad the song when it's sung alone. Unrequited love festers like a raisin in the sun. Is this the way it was supposed to be, lingering tunes bathed with rhythm? It's the reopening of old wounds, lies, and alibis. I don't think so…

The above is what I wanted to say; however, the time and moment have slipped away. Still, I struggle with your persona both night and day, trying to make sense of this comedy. Perhaps you feel the time is moving with each grain. Self-preservation is what's going on today; a game seniors play. I'll always recall a friendship with a smile and will let the truth speak through the words of a song about how I've passed this way before. I'll smile the smile that curled the corners of your mouth. Another door stands before me, long winding paths implore me but this time I know the way.

* * *

Strangers met in shadow, merging silhouettes dancing across an opaque wall. Fantasies ran free, with a taste of wine giving courage to ask a full-figured diva, or perhaps her more graceful slender sister, for a dance. It wouldn't have mattered had the lady said no. Enchanting strains played on like a blue-light special. Women danced and perhaps found a chance for a sweet romance. All one needed to do was ask and snake an arm about the curvy lady's waist. And if she liked you, she would let you know by the ease of her stride. Her body melted into yours and held you against her mound.

Pomade and sweat penetrated the fest. A short, slender lady had me all up in her grill. She straddled my thigh and went down deep. Clutching and holding in guttural sighs; chitterlings, black-eyed peas, potato salad, ribs, yams and collard greens waited. Oh, Baby! Baby, lovers went thigh-to-thigh in grinding to Smokey's Motor City lyrics.

I broke away to get some air when Magnolia Clydesdale appeared. The place was jumping … Another jolt: rum-Coke and passion soared and burst into flames. Men got busy writing numbers and names.

Magnolia Clydesdale hailed from the cornbread basket of the Deep South. "Yes-sir-buddy!" the boys exclaimed, "Love that ponytail without any shame." Her long flowing locks teased the small of her back. Few had trouble recalling her name. Her hips flared like an upright bass fiddle. Her waist was thick but tight around the middle.

"They grow them big on the farm!" another exclaimed. "Probably kept the barnyard gossiping." Back home Maggie would dance, flashing her dazzling white panties—a challenge to those who would dare. Her rich magnolia accent was sweet early-morning molasses running over a stack of steamy buttermilk biscuits. Her hips caused the sofa cushions to sink, taking anything that rolled or was unattached beneath her wide-spreading cheeks. A cigarette butt found its way after being placed in an ancient ashtray. She snuffed the smoldering cinder.

A slow jam played, but Maggie sat this one out, downing a second rum-coke and angling for a third. Her soft brown eyes were all a glow.

The drink hit the mark, getting her ready to do the nasty in the dark. She smiled as I approached, but another had beaten me to the punch. She accepted his hand in the dance. She rose, allowing the hem of her skirt to drift high across her massive thighs where gleaming garter snap fasteners peeked. Maggie chuckled and moved to a familiar strain that began to play. The dancer encircled her thick waist and moved with the stride as his hand drifted. Maggie smiled, eyeing the bulge tenting in his trousers, showing a tell-tale stain shouting to all who cared to know that the man had spewed his seed against the Southern bell's grinding strut.

"You returned, but I hadn't expected it to be this soon," she said, addressing me, the looming shadow, and thinking it was Amos, so I became Amos. "Isn't it about time we got better acquainted?" she asked, adding, "Do we want to tease Wife's suspicion?"

I threw myself upon Maggie's' luscious body: fat thighs slammed. I ground into her swollen crotch. She writhed, with panties being devoured by her quivering ass. I urged her on hands and knees, waiting for her jockey to mount. I came again, grinding into her.

The back of her thighs loomed largely. Maggie wanted an old- fashioned fucking. However, if she persisted, Amos would soon be drained.

This is what she wanted: bust the nut so she could get back to the stranger who did the dip with a slow grinding drop of his hip. Crotch friction and scissoring limbs pumping and pounding fire, desire. We busted nuts. Maggie showed little mercy. She encircled and locked, and we blew again.

"My darling," she whispered in bliss, spicing her tone with a sweet, soft kiss, "Are you through?" Before I could answer, she had slipped into panties and adjusted her girdle, arranged her skirt and left the room permeated with her Southern musk. Maggie had bigger fish to fry. She returned to blue lights fading into a midnight sky. Silhouettes merged into shadows.

Strains continued to play. A slender woman moved closer and remained locked in my arms. Maggie nodded a quick 'HELLO!' The lady drifted with me, finishing a sweet grind. Somehow Maggie got between us—we shared a brief introduction and some lighthearted banter with a Southern drawl. "I like how you dance," she said. "Can you do that in bed?" Our conversation ended too quickly when Maggie chuckled, saying it was time for her to be leaving for the South. "Don't look so sad, Mister," she said. "I'll be moving here later this fall—maybe we can—how do you say it?" "Hookup," I replied, kissing her fingertips and accepting the moment as the last time I would see her. Equating sex with love and love with sex can screw you up. When all was said and done, the saga belonged to Sweet Magnolia.

* * *

Maggie Clydesdale kept her promise. She did move north. Fate must have been smiling the day I ran next door and found Maggie struggling with grocery bags. I couldn't hold back my glee. I shouted a 'Hello!' But I didn't mean to startle, causing groceries to spill across the floor. She stooped to retrieve. A checkered, red and black pleated skirt shimmied into a tight fit. Garter straps caged. I could imagine panties cut through her flesh. Raised impressions showed. Her stomach rounded into a gentle curve, fanning into flaring hips. Big legs and milk bottle ankles perched in leather strap pumps.

Maggie's smile wasn't meant for me. It was more for a boyfriend named Brock and his lumbering steps that announced his presence. A menacing scar streaked his left cheek. Brock eyed me from a six-foot seven-inch body. The bulge from his hulking thighs would part the cheeks of a female elephant backing against his grinding tight denim, stripping the bark from a tree.

Maggie rushed, smothering him with kisses, and appeared to straddle him. Brock could rip a lead door from its hinges. Flesh oozed from his vise-like fingers. Maggie kicked, bit and scratched. He rolled her panties. Hot juices dripped. "Make me beg!" she gasped. He rubbed against her slick fit. "Yes, do me hard," Maggie cried. I thought myself lucky to be so near. However, all I got was a pain for their little game. I stood in torment, aching to take his place. I closed my mind to everything but the stroking of Maggie. Days became weeks, and weeks became months.

Maggie whimpered to Brock's ferocious pounding, "Yes! Yes! I like it rough!" Their bodies clashed in the awful heat, launching Ulysses' mythical passage through the Aegean Sea. His big dick stretched her. "Oh, that's so good!" Maggie moaned, soft and weak. Bedsprings rang; Brock grunted like a stuck monkey just riding that donkey. I tried to ignore but ended up cursing fate.

Their commotion hit the floor. I got out of the bed and onto the fire escape. The heat was stifling. I needed a reprieve from an elusive breeze.

Shadows danced. I peered into the room. The dusky view focused on a writhing mass. Maggie extended her legs and hooked them across Brock's muscled haunches. Shivering and trembling, she kept on kicking. The Clydesdale reared, skewered by a bucking mad donkey. Snorting in unison, they jumped without care. Juices churned into the cream. Brock didn't know he was about to lose his precious dream.

The telephone rang. A pick-up had to be made, and someone's fingers had to be broken. Maggie begged him not to go; she'd make it worth his while. The syndicate wouldn't understand, he said. Maggie knew Brock's dealing in drugs, but humping someone named Betty wasn't part of the deal. Maggie found a note—lipstick stains is how it all began. Brock promised he'd be back. He told her to keep lights off. Brock wanted her when he walked through the door.

No words were spoken between us. Weeks drifted by. She passed me in the lobby, watching me out the corner of her eye, sometimes greeting cordially; I acknowledged.

Her great body kept me guessing 'Why?' She hadn't turned me in or mentioned a word to Brock. My horns were growing; she had to know. However, Maggie gave no indication, nor a hasty last-minute invitation.

Brock eventually returned, wondering why his woman seemed more interested in sleep. Thoughts of Brock were the furthest from her mind. A tingling still rang. Something was amiss. It started with a kiss. He assumed she was seeing someone. Maggie countered with: "Who's Betty?" They were arguing, fighting like an old couple.

Brock wanted it one way, but Maggie said no—that he had to go. Brock was determined to win her back. He had severed ties with Betty, but it was too late. "You are trying to get under my skin!" Maggie bellowed. "This is one fight you aren't going to win!"

Yet Brock was doing the talking and wasn't about to make like a tree and leave. He slipped an arm around her waist. He crushed his hard body against hers. "Not this time," Maggie quipped. "You're hurting me." There was one way he would listen. The more she resisted, the more it tortured his fevered brain.

"We had our good time. Get on with your life, and I'll get on with mine," Maggie pleaded. Whatever they had had been replaced. "Who's the punk?" he asked with a snarl.

"What does it matter?" Maggie replied. "We're through."

"We're never through," he said, eyes ablaze in searing red. "I'll leave nothing for him!" A slip of a zipper, trousers hit the floor. A lamp slammed against a wall. Hulking bodies tumbled to the ground. The front door slammed. Thrashing steps exploded in the outside hall. "Don't bother to call."

Maggie apologized for the commotion the other night. She was returning from another day on the job. She got rid of Brock but said it wasn't right for us to get it on—it was just too soon. However, she knew how to dance. "You owe me," she reminded.

Some wine and a familiar strain—Smokey was crooning once again. Buttermilk biscuits baking in the oven ignited a grind with a whole lot of shoving. She reminded me of a recent promise to honor Brock's memory. She discarded all of that with her blouse and skirt. Her bra and a garter strap spandex girdle held firm. Sculpted thighs bulged like a female Olympic sprinter. She backed into my lap, fulfilling a fantasy about grappling with a massive girdled rump. She pushed. Black-eyed peas—the pot was boiling. Maggie straddled and ground against my knee. Her sweet Southern musk captured me.

Her girdle cut into my groin with a waistband scraping my balls. Friction is burned. The room was smoking. I became more fascinated with how girdles encased a fleshy behind—keeping the goodness bounded before the eventual explosion. Some way I was going to split her girdle, get between those fat thighs, and drive until I heard her cry out. She squirmed and said, "Unsnap my garters first!"

"What about Brock?"

"Chill the thought!" she replied. "He doesn't have to know." I struggled to unsnap those damned garter straps. Each release sent a fluttering spike to the center of my loins from the arching pressure of her globular spheres. My hands stayed busy at her pendulous orbs, awesome thighs, and one more strap to unfasten. I held back with her shifting in my lap. I was about to explode. Another moment more and I'd sure have made a fool of myself.

She mercifully faced me in releasing bra snap fasteners. Her nipples bored into my chest. I tweaked her nipples before fastening teeth to the tender morsels. Maggie gasped and shivered, stretching her arms above her head. A familiar fragrance teased for a sultry moment that stirred deep within.

"You can't get into me this way," she moaned. "Take off my girdle." She shifted and bruised against my grinding at her. I managed the tight spandex down massive Olympic sprinter thighs. Arms encircled and hands cupped pendulous orbs. I pounded and rubbed into her girdled behind. Maggie pushed back; we collapsed in visions of summer afternoons behind the barn. Maggie bellowed in a buttermilk tone, "I like how you dance." I slowed the pace to get more leverage into her; she extended across a bale of hay and lifted me, settling into my lap.

She held me deep. I teetered at an alarming rate— just getting ready to bust a nut. I repeatedly stabbed into her, hoping she was near because I wasn't going to last much longer.

"Oh! Oh! Oh! Fill me," she sighed. "Slam it!" I found leverage when I mounted by planting my knees in the back hollow of her own. Tears welled. Hips jerked in a bucking frenzy. Maggie implored, "Don't take it out!" Deep from the loins the cream began to bubble. Buttermilk splashed! Maggie turned on to her back with scissoring limbs. I held her in a perfect 'W' bathing her walls with my scalding seed. Our bodies rumbled and then exploded in sweet unison.

Brock had lost his prize. A pounding at the door matched the writhing across the floor. He had returned, spewing his venom. But the cops were after him. They wrestled him to the ground and slapped on cuffs. There wasn't much more. Maggie opened her front door. All Brock saw was her grinding hams and lust-clouded eyes. There was no holding back. Her girdle, reduced to a spandex cord, gripped the backs of her thighs. I rested upon the knotted elastic cable in slingshot tension, the arrow poised and about to fly, once more striking her mossy peeking bull's-eye.

Hot juices cascaded down thick, quivering thighs. She bobbed, betraying all trust. "You're hard! Make me beg!" I grabbed her hips. "Oh yes, that's it! It feels good!" I was humping that ass, just going with the flow. Smokey continued to croon. Maggie got all dizzy and weak in the knees. She arched a little higher. I rode each bounce; we slumped to the floor, marking the last time I ever cursed Fate.

Dance Tonight

I want to dance tonight
Until the broad daylight;
Sigh,
Cry
To an Ephemeral strain,
Deliberate and slow.
Writhing hips and scissoring limbs—
A fervent surge;
Quivering flesh and the cervix shift,
A tight snug fit.
Orgasmic tremors like a taut silk thread.
Teased,
Ragged, jagged in short heaves,
Fluttering limbs lifting me higher;
Her musk permeates with wild desire.

The wine had a way of freeing inhibitions. Our conversation covered everything from size to the best way to please a woman.

Truth flowed like water through a leaking bucket. She pranced about the apartment. Thoughts of riding her across the arm of a well- padded sofa made me weak with anticipation.

Angela stripped to a black spandex body suit. "This is how I warm up," she said, awakening from a long, sweet sleep. Her sudden burst kept me wondering what was in the wine that had her doing jumping jacks and cartwheels on the floor. I couldn't help feeling I had to impress her—that the Brotherhood extended across the Nation, driven by an obsession with Eve's descendant.

Nevertheless, it was Angela's turn to command. She took the lead with subtle incantations to be repeated. "Don't be coy. Join me!" she said. Soon I was naked to the waist and bouncing in my briefs. I did a few jacks of my own. "Sit-ups," she barked. I clasped her ankles. She began the count. Soon we changed positions. I wasn't about to let her show me up.

Spasms ripped. I hoped she hadn't noticed me breaking the wind, passing gas like a pair of pants being torn, without skipping a beat. Angela smiled in announcing, "Push-ups!" I followed when she turned onto her stomach and ground into the thick pile carpeting. Hot, sweaty routines turned her on. Before she could get to five, I had draped myself across her quivering backside. I humped her deep, shadowy, spandex-shielded crevice that rebounded like a trampoline. "No! Not yet," she sighed. "Lick me." She had to be kidding—that coarse-ass girdle would've stripped my tongue. I undid the snaps. She wanted me to go slow and so I did it her way by drawing her closer with a well- manicured hand. I took a comfortable position between her legs. This was going to take time and I was going to enjoy it.

I continued stroking and licking. She began to squirm. I inserted two fingers, palm side up. About an inch to two inches inside the entrance, I could feel a round, roughened pea. It began to enlarge with smooth and constant stroking pressure. I stroked that sweet spot. Her breath came in short gasps.

"Oh! Oh! You're good!" she said, taking hold of my ears and ripping me to my feet, urging me higher until my thighs were at her breasts and I was sitting on her chest. She swallowed and got really sloppy about it, sucking and slurping for all she was worth and more. She had my eyes rolling to the top of my head. Her knees rose and thumped my ass, pushing me forward and deep into her gullet. She squeezed and slithered a finger into me. All sensations were about to break; I gritted my teeth— ready to pop. Instead, I pulled back and hoisted her limbs, urging her thighs against her breasts. She gushed opened like a ripe split grape. "Oh baby," Angela moaned when I sank to the hilt and ground against her mound. Squirming and twisting from side to side, her thighs held me fast. I cupped her ass and plunged. "Ooh! Ooh! You're so damned good!" she whined, rotated and slithered along to the harpooning. Her arms floated above and away from her body. Her head swayed and eyes rolled to the plunge. Her body stiffened in a sudden and upward rolling thrust and gave passage for the boat that was engulfed between her full-sized thighs.

Spying

. . Her perception was oblivious to how weight, strategically placed, complemented a more passionate appeal … threats of judgment day's sentencing couldn't stop me from admiring Bernice's magnificently sculpted body. I continued to debate with family values that fiercely defended—that she was Uncle Bertrand's

Twoman. My alter-ego, Shane, took a stand among the chaos to confirm my innocence and to finally settle the argument that Uncle Bertrand's marriage hadn't been consummated. Bernice was not yet family, and until then I was spared damnation, until Bernice caught me studying her broad rump.

A song cried about being too young for women. I ignored such heartfelt lyrics because they didn't apply to me, or so I thought until epiphany came slashing like a stiletto with the whimpering of a woman's sigh from behind my uncle's bedroom door. Was it a cry of fear or pleasure? Bernice had paraded before her fiancé with gyrating hips and a grinding hot ass that threatened the seams to her spandex garter strap girdle. Thigh-high nylons framed her large, shapely limbs. I kept reminding myself that Bernice was not a blood relative and that it was all right to look. However, assurance was not guaranteed. Religious doctrines had me floundering with my nineteen years and a willingness to take my uncle's place.

I imagined him caressing his woman; my mind's eye watched him clumsily inch her skirt above her broad, writhing hips. Thoughts framing incestuous notions rushed. Knowing that I might burn in Hell for what I was thinking, I continued to debate my innocence with a conscience that became more unforgiving. It fiercely maintained that the lusty Bernice was Uncle Bert's woman. However, Shane's voice rose from the chaos, finally acknowledging Bert's marriage, but like a sword that cut both ways, he also reminded me that Bernice was not of the blood. It stood; a protective barrier—neither Shane nor I will be judged too harshly and perhaps be granted a reprieve. However, what redemption didn't give, Shane stole.

Bernice was at least fifteen years older than I, although I had turned nineteen. Her stature and grace made her appear much wiser. I marveled at how she wore age like a crown. I ravished her in my dreams. Aunt Bernice could whip up a batch of smothered chicken, candied yams, potato salad and collard greens like no one else. Dessert was a refreshing taste of banana pudding that had family slipping to the front of the line for that last scoop. She seemed to enjoy the attention, particularly her smile in tune to the billowing action beneath her skirt that had blind men talking about seeing again. She felt their hungry gaze when retrieving a casserole from the lowest rung of the oven. And yet with the mind games, a refuge in a monastery would have been a good idea and a safe haven for me had it not led through Bernice's bedroom.

Her fullness offered comfort against cold winter evenings, and a particular young man would be lying had he pretended not to notice. However, Shane saw. Despite his crudeness, he was honest and quite direct. I couldn't help admiring him; although we shared the same skin, at times, I hated him. Shane was everything I wasn't: He burst from the depths of an overly active libido with a song about being too old for girls and finally too young for Bernice. Shane left out the part about trying to get next to her would mean selling out my good Uncle Bertrand for his forgetting to close the bedroom door. It sent me on a roller-coaster ride I had been trying to get off. Bernice raised her skirt to a garter strap fastener securing thigh-high nylons to a well-stuffed panty girdle. I stood in the shadows. Bertrand slipped the fabric to the back of her large tanned thighs in a tantalizing move, ever so slow.

I went to sleep dreaming that I strummed my fingers across her belly. I ground against her with long, enduring strokes to evoke the sleeping passion she aroused in me.

Aunt Bernice grew aware of my dilemma concerning family morals and her. But with a cruel smile, she appeared to be taunting. This play between us continued for years, only this time I nearly stumbled into a trash bin. She thought it amusing. "What you looking at?" she would ask when catching me studying her thick body. Shane reminded that things happen for a reason, although I would have to grab fate by the throat to find humor in my being clumsy. "Better keep your hands in your pocket, and your zipper zipped," she teased. "Just don't let me catch you with your skirt below your knees if you please," Shane answered. I prayed there would be more to this game than me always ending up as the pawn.

Shane understood my struggles with religion, philosophies and the price that would surely keep me from getting into Heaven. However, Shane insisted that these tenets were mere interpretations of God's laws where a man was the author.

Nothing happened with me that night. Nevertheless, it did for Bertrand. The coroner transported his body to the county morgue. The guilt returned that evening, in a voice I barely recognized: Shane begging Aunt Bernice to sleep with him. Shane was out of control and had to be restrained when Bernice suddenly relented. "What's stopping you?"

Another dream where all pretenses got smothered by wet, steamy kisses and strumming fingers across her soft belly. Shane assumed control. Bernice held to the sleeping passion that came alive in the cries bursting from her throat. She took me between her thick flailing limbs. She locked her thick legs around my waist. Spasms quaked; thick cream streamed like a knotted silk cable drawn through me and summoning convulsions to a bittersweet cacophony of pleasure. We rumbled across a hardwood floor behind a locked bedroom door. Love flowed and then exploded in an infinite passage of inane adjectives and flashing lights.

I recalled how sacred scriptures blocked a student from getting that old-school booty. . . Bernice's ample physique became a holy dilemma when Uncle Bertrand introduced her to the family. She had men stuffing old used socks into a jock to impress her. She stood five feet eight in heels but appeared to tower above me, although our eyes met on a level plane. Even so, a consortium of contradictions followed: I was taller, although she towered, perched in stilettos. "You're short for your age but cute," she said upon her introduction. She seemed to be sizing me up, but for what purpose? I didn't have a clue. Her sweet sandalwood fragrance stirred fantasies that were everything but quiet. The whisper of her graceful scissoring limbs became her calling card that seemed to say, "Try me! What you're saving it for?" I had no answer, but I was through with stuffing jocks with old socks to impress. I was about to give up on chance when during a family reunion Bernice had a beef with Uncle Bertrand. They had argued all the way from Baton Rouge, Louisiana to Richmond, Virginia. I blessed my good fortune when Bertrand stormed out and booked himself in a local motel, leaving Bernice alone. The incident led to my sharing a bed with the big-legged diva. It became a night when innocence got lost in a storm. "It's time to get some booty," Shane seemed to be saying.

The crowded family compound had one bedroom available, the same one promised me because I was the oldest of three sons. Bernice didn't give it a second thought. She stripped to a half-slip, muttering something about getting back at Bertrand. I pretended to be asleep. She toppled into bed, catapulting me against her fully stuffed, open- crotch, panty-girdled behind. "Don't even think it! You're just a baby!" Had she forgotten I was nineteen? What right did she have to claim my bed and then treat me like a child? I wanted her out. Bernice didn't wait for hospitality to be offered; she took it. "Watch those hands, Sugar," she warned, "or you'll be explaining why your arm is in a sling." She had to go!

Bernice was soon muttering how she was going to get back at Bertrand. Her thick ass claimed the better part of the bed and left me teetering. For now, I wouldn't bother with confronting her, for it was getting cold—a confluence of ironies. The awkwardness became lustful excitement that encompassed the seven deadly sins where obsession became the final dagger. I draped my body across her broad behind. She didn't move when I ground against her. The greater the pressure meant the greater the warmth. Despite my early misgivings, it wasn't a bad idea having her near. It became a win-win situation that could frighten her with a bold commitment to slipping that girdle from her voluptuous body. I climbed the high arching slope, a frictionless glide against her slip setting me firmly on top. The only fighting was against a nut-busting orgasm. I strained against that fat behind where the open-crotch panty girdle rolled halfway up and across her lush cheeks. Contractions twitched in her great divide. She instinctively arched higher while massaging and tightening about me. I stumbled again, but this time remained draped across her back. Delicious sensations erupted when my groin slipped beneath the hem to her girdle and into her snug cavern. I was about to cum when a sudden wrenching snapped me from her. Bernice was suddenly awake. I expected her demand for what, when, where, why or how questions to end with her referring to me as a no-good bastard. Instead, she whispered for me to come closer. Any closer and I would have been under her.

She guided me between her big legs. "Don't be afraid," she said in a dry, halting whisper. Was I still dreaming? I felt her hand on the back of my head, urging me into her gaping caldron. "Oh yes!" she said, bathing my face in her musk. Mother Earth opened in the morning sun and took me in. Her limbs encircled me. I reeled in her liquid fire. She drummed her heels against my buttocks, moving as if climbing a tree. Friction awakened every sense to a shifting, slithering and slurping fit. She repeatedly called, "Nice and steady!" She murmured face down and ass high. Passion dribbled along her inner thigh. She grinned with a deep, satisfied sigh, uttering, "No one must ever know." She knew I had been watching when she had been with Uncle Bertrand, but offered no scolding. Instead, she arched a little higher. I had yet to be punished. "That's what you get for spying on me," she said, closing the door and abandoning me to the shadows. Later I discovered how cheating, destroyed one's trust, but I was the last to be throwing stones. She explained the how Bertrand had been seeking other women; he was never satisfied, she said. Barroom philosophers reasoned it was man's nature to cheat. Bertrand soon passed, leaving Bernice the caretaker of his legacy stashed between their bedroom mattresses. In spite of all, she felt close to him, more so in death.

Upon a visit, I had discovered the collection, a long black dildo peeking from between Bernice's bedroom mattress, along with Bertrand's glossy magazines. I was transfixed by one model that greatly resembled Bernice when she announced, "It's bedtime!" Upon entering my room without knocking, her tone changed when she saw the toys. "Who gave you the right?" I had violated a spiritual link between her and Bertrand. Sharing had held them together during quiet moments when the inevitable loomed in the shadows. He often questioned the love she gave to him, although she never gave cause for his jealousy. "I should tell your parents how you've been rummaging through my husband's belongings," she said with a glare. "Don't," I begged. "I was just curious."

"Still looking for sugar?" she asked with a spiced Sunday morning smile. Nylons hissed; she strolled with answers in the wake of her scissoring thighs and crying bedsprings from the night before. I was always near to catch her cruel smile. Passion surfaced in an infinite throbbing that seemed to mock me. Her stocking legs flailed. "You want?"

Her broad hips and donkey ass, encased in garter belts, stockings, half-slips and an open-crotch panty girdle, taunted me for years. "You're not much taller from what I remembered," she said, trying to make conversation. She was still intimidating but refined with streaks of gray.

Daily labor had blessed her with a body of a woman half her age would die for. And I told her so. "That's enough out of you, young man," she said, blushing while preparing for a Saturday night bath. Crisis averted, I thought with relief, tiptoeing past her open door. She leafed through the magazine. Her denim skirt rose high across her well-muscled limbs stretched across the bed, "Does this excite you?" she asked, addressing an empty chair. "I can feel your hands," she said, cupping her breasts.

"It's what you want, isn't it, Bertrand? Well, I want it too," she said, producing a short, stout dildo and slipping the tip into her. She worked her fingers into her anus, moaning into a trance. She turned the page. The pocket-sized jockey mounted the Clydesdale, easing the dildo between huge ass cheeks. Bernice grunted with fingers immersed. She worked that jockey. The dildo paled with the realization that summer vacation was going to be interesting.

Bernice went about her chores wearing a housecoat that sculpted and teased with scenes from the evening before. "Is there something wrong?" she barked, catching me studying her. "I am not telling your parents, if that's what you're thinking," she said referring to my discovery. She asked if I had been serious about her—that she was more attractive than the glossy centerfold.

"I wouldn't lie," I said, rising from the table hiding a stiff intuition that had a mind of its own. She laughed, saying I needed to get ready for bed—that it was late. I moved but brushed against her. We were passing through a small alcove. Bernice held her position far too long for the move to be accidental. She surrounded me. I slipped and stuttered enjoying the fit. "Sugar, this is wrong," she cried. "You need someone your own age." She reminded me that we weren't blood related, yet the feelings we had for each other would not leave this house.

Sunday service was the best show in town. Many of the city's finest women, decked out in tight-fitting pastels, were present. It seemed that all were accustomed to hard labor. There wasn't a 'bow- wow' in the bunch. The church deacons were quick to notice Aunt Bernice. "Sorry about Bertrand," they said. "You have a beautiful aunt," someone said. "Were you jealous?" Bernice asked as we drove home. We pulled along the side of the road. "Take the wheel," she said with a wink. Soon we were swerving, driving everywhere but in a straight line. I got the hang of it. "My, it's hot for this time of day," she said, hiking her skirt higher across her garter snap fasteners, giving a view of how the garter straps cut into her thighs. She released the clasps. "What a relief," she sighed. A great burden had been set free.

"Did you like what you saw?" I didn't know where this was leading. "Don't be coy with me," she said. "Last night! You were outside my door."

I started swerving again. "Easy," she said reaching across my lap for the wheel. "That's it baby, steady." We drove along in silence. The heat and her rose musk fragrance had my head spinning. "You need a beautiful girl your age," she reminded me. I agreed, for this woman was too much for me. "Let me get back to being your aunt." This was fine because I wasn't about to make a fool of myself again, trying to get close to a mature, God-fearing femme-fatale, who happened to be my late uncle's wife! She was right; I needed someone my age.

"Morning comes sooner than it does in the city," she said, insisting we retire. Reluctantly I agreed, stepping from the shower. She burst in on me and had me scampering for a towel; Bernice was quicker. She wore a short black thigh-length robe. "I need your opinion," she said, peeling the garment from her shoulders. She stretched across my bed in red panties with the matching bra, garter belt and thigh highs. "It's for a gentleman. Do you think he'll like it?" "He'll split your panties,"

I said, jealousy gnawing at the pit of my stomach. Whoever, or whatever, if this was her idea of a joke, I failed to see the humor.

"Don't just stand there," she said, taking control. "Don't you think it's time we finished what we started?" Instead of feeling excited, I became cautious. It was the first mention of our affair since we had been together. "Come! Don't you think we've waited long enough?" It had been haunting me despite denial, and maybe it was doing the same to her. "Passion makes liars of all of us," she said, stripping the towel from my waist. "I've waited too long," she whispered. We were in the bed grunting like beasts in heat. Stockings lay in threads. Garter belt snap fasteners scratched me; she guided me into her. We drifted into each other, satiated in an obscene tangle of arms and legs. "It's so good," she inhaled. Orgasms ripped and we drifted off into sleep and didn't awake until well past noon.

Summer passed and soon it was time to return to the city somewhat wiser, more appreciative. That winter I received a gift, a glossy magazine wrapped in an ugly brown envelope with no return address marked 'Personal'. There was a note attached stating:

Sugar,

You left your magazine. Hmm, you need to be punished. See you next summer,

Aunt Bernice

Camp Bliss

. . She flaunted a generous endowment until realizing the store didn't carry her size . . .

"Make hay while the sun shines!" And so, we did, Cassidy and I, better known as Sundance. We had just turned eighteen, living for the moment with little regard for history, and had long since decided to let the future take care of itself. Graffiti marred posters, park benches, and tenement hallways cited our schemes. We were primed for a lifetime behind bulletproof glass and steel curtains. We didn't know it, or better yet, we just didn't give a damn.

That's when Justice summoned us like a wise old farmer separating weeds from the harvest. He declared it a greater crime for youth to be spending the rest of their days counting water spots on a wall with bunkmate Bruno forever lurking in the shadows. Sentencing struck with a pounding gavel. A six-month makeover at Camp Bliss was in order.

Before we knew it, we were boarding a metro-liner headed for the wilderness, far removed from a city that never slept. Yet a few of us would admit that we were at fault—that we got what we deserved. There lay our redemption, the metro-liner surging into the valley. Lofty oaks, spruces, and evergreens shrouded the earth with shadows as mountains loomed. I was fascinated by a Bull Moose. He stalked a sloe-eyed cow nibbling at crisp grass morsels. “She’s setting him up,” the ticket collector said, and with a chuckle he added, “Just like a woman; she got that Bull Moose hooked and he doesn’t know it!” All was in tune with Nature’s plan. In a single bound, the bull mounted the broad rear. He kept on humping, all the while stumbling to maintain his gait.

It reminded me of plans I had with sweet Phyllis. She declared I was her man but not to be disappointed if she’s ‘knocking boots’ with someone else when I’m gone. Phyllis kept things real. It was her way of keeping me out of jail and warning suitors she belonged to me. The thought kept me loyal, but she knew me too well—that threat would last for a short while. Losing her was a matter of time. Rather keeping the door closed to our relationship, she added that I shouldn’t believe all that I hear and half of what I see. It was like the first time we met and I caught her being saddled during a nut sack- slapping, ass-riding orgy. Damned if she didn’t growl!

Yet she was in control, gripping that sack so the rider couldn’t bust a nut. Pleasure assailed, her grip growing tighter. Lord, there was no quit just like the cow with the Bull Moose settling in. The rider became bug-eyed and out of his wits waiting for her to slip into a nervous fit. She kept on churning. Phyllis’s thick bouncing haunches set off a blaze in the brother’s pants! The rider once boasted at how he could make women squeal!

“Is that how you feel?” Phyllis asked with a smirk and then hopped on his dick, sliding along his length. She clenched and creamed all up and down his pole. She ground into his lap and crushed his nuts before smothering him. She lifted high and then descended. He was at her mercy, slithering in her creamy stream. Juices bubbled and overflowed in a toe-curling frenzy. The rider was in his glory stroking that G-spot into another frictionless burn. Orgasms teased with spasms throbbing in rapid succession that hurt, but it was hurting really good. He was the winner, tearing up that ramp! True to his boast he made her skeet with curling toes! And when it was done, he lay there at her feet. She gripped him and held firm. "Steady darling!" she instructed in a sultry tone. "You aren't going home." She fed her opulent tits. "It was just the first nut, and you got more work to do! So don't make me slap you, because I will!"

I had to move on and not think about who would be getting it next. And for where I was headed it didn't matter—at least for now. "'Jody got my girl and was gone!" Bittersweet farewells were made of this. Phyllis and I parted with a long, endearing kiss. I was sure to miss holding, sculpting and molding that booty in one last feel. My life was headed in the wrong direction when Justice stepped in with a remedy that would play out in a federally funded forest conservation camp. The resurrection without discretion had me wondering 'How?'

"Community Service," the judge decreed. He was doing us a favor, but we didn't know it then. Cassidy and I packed our bags and moved into daylight that faded into shadows where silence ushered sweet mysteries to an evening surging in the valley. The Bull was still whaling that cow. She backed him into her cave.

Nature's wonders were meant to be shared, not harnessed, spared, or released. The conservation project called for the swiftness of feet and a purse-snatching hand.

The campsite waited for the new recruits. Angular features contorted with arrogance made the campsite's taskmaster more intimidating than she had to be. We referred to her as Ethel. "She took after her father," I dared to mention to Cassidy. Somehow, she got wind of it and I ended up doing the latrine. Her reputation for breaking balls rang throughout the camp, but I had to be the first victim. Cassidy just grinned. He had better luck in the evening, passing an open window where the sound of a busted steam pipe turned out to be Ethel.

But being secluded in these mountains had everyone wishing: Let me do it —show them love. "The way she pinched her nipples was a crime," Cassidy replied, adding, "The funny thing about it all was that she was calling your name!"

"Tell me anything," I said, thinking how she reminded me of Phyllis. Women would make you lean to see how far you would go and then step back and watch you fall.

"But that's because she likes you," Cassidy defended.

"Being mean made her twitch!" I said, realizing how Big Ethel's stroking proved lust didn't always come with delicate features.

Ethel held total control, guiding us in turning the soil. Plain hard work showed in a well-toned physique and for women such strenuous routines made the backbone healthy and ripe for birthing babies. Still, it would have helped had Ethel smiled. In fact, the only time she laughed was when assigning details that added hours to an ordinary workday. I was reminded that women were like a three-dimensional cube drawing: the more one focused, the more the picture shifted with Phyllis and of course, Ethel. Cassidy and I were trapped.

When we reported for orientation Ethel was on her knees hunting for her contact lens. Her skirt covered so little of her ass. It was quite a show. It draped across her broad hips, framing her thick ass encased in black gossamer panties. "How dare you barge in without knocking?" she snapped. But I wasn't listening. And though she was the careless one, Cassidy and I were going to pay for the view. We were assigned to her special projects team.

My joy was in imagining her puckered brown eye and how I'd poke it and watch it bounce back. I would make her squeal! I couldn't get over how she tucked her thick ass, leaping to her feet at the touch of the door knob. "It's brains you don't have," she answered with her swollen treasure tucked between her shapely thighs, but now I became the hound, having little need for rules or protocol! Yet reluctant because of that stiff right hand she brandished and demanded, I left but paused for a moment, eyeing the swell below my belt loop.

"You have size," she said. "It doesn't matter," she continued. "You aren't getting any!" Still, she brushed against me. "Forget what you saw."

My horns got longer; Ethel's presence became more endearing. Just thinking about it had me on the verge of losing my mind. I was all ablaze, aching to test that sweet live wire. There was no end to what I would've done had I got Ethel alone. But I wasn't the only one eager to carry out this mission. Cassidy told how he lay awake thinking about getting trapped between her bone-crushing limbs. I wished him luck, knowing that we will always be rivals.

Ethel managed well keeping us in line so as not to disturb the countryside while carrying out society's mandate in a last-ditch effort at rehabbing this motley crew.

Grinding haunches wreaked havoc to an ancient blood oath to fraternity and brotherhood. Cassidy's good looks and sweet words often won the prize. But this time Cassidy's sugar-coated greetings were rewarded with a cold stare. Whatever he was selling, Ethel wasn't buying. Yet I couldn't gloat. She smiled at me when dishing out assignments nobody wanted. And since Cassidy was never chosen, he took it as a favorable sign Ethel had something more personal with him in mind. It prompted his brag about how it was a matter of time. But her indifference told another story. It became anyone's guess who was winning this contest. Whoever she was smiling at, it wasn't him. Yet barroom philosophers often warned to be aware of that which lies beneath the surface.

Backbreaking routines continued to fall into my lap. Campsite landscaping and hedge sculpting—making a willow grow was part of this picture. That scrawny bush was on life support, needing someone to pull the plug. I unzipped to give it a final baptismal. But for whatever reason I found the pond. Even the weak deserved a second chance, just as the most pathetic earned a reprieve. It dawned on me that perhaps this was the reason the Judge's decree had us marking the wilderness—a second chance.

I recalled a story about a man trapped in a storm. The flood was rising; the man retreated to his front step. A boat passed by, the man refusing to get in, saying, "I'm all right. The Lord will save me." A second boat passed, but by this time the man stood perched on his chimney top. Again, his answer was the same. He refused for the last time. When he arrived at the Pearly Gates, he asked the Lord, "Why didn't you save me?" The Lord replied,

"Who do you think sent the boats?"

"Move that boulder and smooth the soil," Ethel snapped. She had been watching all along: "Water the willow and it will grow." Through Ethel's manner seemed hard and exacting, she showed another side I hadn't expected to find: a rare appreciation for beauty that radiated from within. She said dreams were like a sapling willow. Nourish it daily and it will grow. Purpose and belief tooled the Taskmaster's hand to make this land. All we had to do was follow his plan.

Still, half the campsite was in awe of her physique. Cassidy continued plotting how he would get her in bed—thinking his task would be easy. Nothing was sacred to Cassidy when it meant spying on Ethel. Thoughts rushed in a lopsided soliloquy whenever she took a trip to the loo. "Hairy what?" He could see a thick bush. Yet after a little clipping it wasn't hairy as it could be! She kept it trimmed, adding a touch that proved exquisite.

There was little to say other than giving thanks to Christmas for coming early.

"That fat sweet pie," Cassidy did sigh, telling his tale to all who would listen, "Mighty pleasing to the eye!" But Ethel caught him. He offered an alibi: "I wasn't looking!" Yet one would have to be blind not to see. What could have been tastier than forbidden fruit? Those thighs were open, with panties at the ankles and a skirt drawn high across her thigh. Ethel closed her legs when she heard him choking.

"What you going to do? Suck it 'til I spew all over your shoe?" Once exposed, the deed was done.

"I didn't see you blink," Cassidy said. "I wasn't looking," he protested. "What more can I say?"

"That's just it," Ethel replied with a smirk. "How did you know it was hairy? And why are you bulging?"

Cassidy had little choice but to confess: "Yes, I lied!" Ethel saw he was horny. Time away from civilization made all appreciate what was near, including a thick wobbling ass with angular features. Yet she showed little mercy, although she took his attention as a compliment. Perhaps that's why Ethel chose to stay in the wilderness. She replied, "That's a shame because you aren't going to get any either." Ethel slipped into her panties after spreading her fat cheeks all in his face.

"You're COLD!" he whined.

She looked at him with amazement. "Boy, you must be crazy! Hit the road!

You aren't getting any." The door slammed at his back. Cassidy ran to a side window and got a peek. Ethel slipped her fingers deep, legs spread wide to a fervent shove. Ethel saw Cassidy standing nearby. "You know that isn't fair!" Cassidy said. She laughed and told him to go. "Go on and stare," is what she said! He got a good look at a twitching twat!

My second-place finish became in a three-dimensional drawing of a cube: It was all about a woman's mindset. Whenever a man thought he had a fix on a woman's persona, it shifted into another form. It appeared Cassidy had gained the lead. And though he proved rude and crude, Ethel seemed to like it.

One could count on Cassidy to give a full account concerning Ethel's beauty eclipsing a cheap bar stool. Despite my new awareness, I couldn't deny what Ethel possessed attracted and made up for a face that would never appear on the cover of Vogue. I avoided her, pretending not to see. Gaining respect was the last thing she should have expected from me. But Cassidy insisted if he pushed the right buttons, she would be his for the taking—that it would require the right situation.

Well, it didn't take long for the situation to arise: The counselor's quarters caught fire and burned to the ground.

Inmates were forced to double up. But luck was with me. I had discovered a cabin hidden in the thick underbrush. As it turned out, that hidden cabin was where Ethel had taken favorites for a taste of discipline spiced with soulful absolution. Earthy musk still lingered. With some tarpaulin, plywood, nails and a hammer, this case was closed. I was able to get an old cluttered fireplace to work in time to meet a sudden drop in temperature. It rained. I found blankets and went to sleep.

It's been said dreams foretell the future. But such ideas didn't come without a price. Demons had a way of lurking in shadows. Cassidy's obsession with Ethel stole its way into my sleep. Yet I couldn't stop thinking about Phyllis. A short-skirted, grieving pony plodded into the room. Muscled flanks vibrated with each step. She stood spread-eagled with hands braced against the wall. "What are you going to do about it?" she asked. It was just a dream, matching the fury of the storm.

Reality played. Ethel, the pony in the short-skirt dream, had wandered into the cabin. She crumpled a letter from a fiancé who changed his mind. This didn't bode well. A scorned woman didn't take prisoners. "What are you doing here?" Ethel snapped. "These are my quarters!" She looked around, noticing the improved setting.

"Who gave you the right?" she rambled. I had expected gratitude. I didn't deserve this. Whether Ethel liked it or not, we were locked in for the night. She threw a chair and would have taken the footlocker had it not been bolted. My better judgment sent me rushing for the front door. But my tired, aching body wouldn't let me move. I held my ground and slept with one eye open, ready for a psychotic hazing.

Fury stormed. Yet it couldn't match Ethel's. "Get out!" she insisted. Yet there was no place to go. And I wasn't about to double- up with Cassidy!

I said it was okay to cry. "I don't need your sympathy," she quipped. Tears streamed down her cheeks.

"Who in their right mind would name a child Roscoe?" I asked, "He doesn't deserve you."

"What makes you an expert?" "I've been through the war."

"I'm sure you have," Ethel replied. But she relented. "Stay until morning," she said stripping and muttering about getting back at Roscoe. A half-slip clung to wide flaring hips sculpting that thick ass. Her feet were perched in laced calf sandals. Her eyes narrowed in warning that I had better not be watching. Ethel tumbled into bed with an awful thud. Her weight had me cornered.

The fireplace was ablaze, transforming coal into dying embers. I moved back. But she moved forward until a massive rear nestled in my lap. She held firm. I grooved between those gigantic spheres. The bunk strained beneath our weight. We were like spoons in a kitchen drawer.

"Baby," Ethel said with a slight laugh, "you had better get back to your side!" Yet she was the intruder. She tossed rules about hospitality out the front door in seizing her corner of the cot.

But damn! Ethel had an ass! I couldn't help admiring her girth. Curiosity ran wild. She nudged me to the edge. "Watch those fingers. Or you'll have a tough time explaining how your finger got a dislocated knuckle." Soon she was asleep.

Weeks of denial spurred passion's rush. Despite the warning, I flipped her slip, exposing a well-muscled behind. Her stuffed baby blues were all that separated. I hooked a leg over the back of a thigh and slid her panties beneath my balls, leaving me like an arrow poised in the tension of an elastic waistband. It became a soulful grind into quaking spheres. I oozed quicksilver, dampening the narrow fabric strip shielding. She arched into a hair-fringed crevice. I settled in the trough of mountainous cheeks. Tremors rushed. It was cold in that cabin. I readied with an alibi should she awake to ask why. But she didn't utter a word. Cassidy's guilt: Ethel was getting even.

All became hazy, with eyes narrowing into slits. "Can you handle me?" she asked. I jumped that thick roast. She bucked like a mad bull. I held fast. She cussed me, slapped to break free. Burning sensations had my bladder in knots, begging release. My sphincter twitched with a sudden blood surge. I fought to hold back. I fastened my lips to Ethel's trembling gash. Her eyes lurched. Tongues slithered. Another slap! But the slap got muffled with thighs pounding in my head. "Baby, you're good," she did growl. I had unleashed a demon. "Oh yes!" Ethel cried, moving to get away. But I held fast and continued to feast, drawing a delicious elixir from her shivering body.

I rose from opened thighs and ground against a swollen mound. She lifted me higher. Our lips touched. Teeth clashed. I moaned in the throes of scissoring limbs climbing across my hips and the pleasure she was giving. "Think fast! Think fast!" I straddled and grappled with her astounding strength. Her cream bubbled and oozed to my slapping nut sack. I held against the inevitable but was about to give in. Ethel gaspingly implored, "No! Not yet! Not yet!" I pulled out and then surged to the pleasure of her grinding.

Breasts went flat against my chest and spilled beneath armpits. Nails dug into my back. She clutched and scratched, challenging the dam that was about to burst. "Now!" she urged. I broke free, ravaging her like a man spreading a vat of butter. Eyes fluttered. We cried in unison. Orgasms ripped. She went limp with eyes still aflutter. Exhausted, I collapsed, impaled, slithering deeper into her tight, snug fit. Limbs entwined. We drifted into the shadows.

The next morning Roscoe became history and Cassidy had to do the latrine. I arose and got busy without being told. The willow was growing high. There were acres left to be cleared. I looked forward to completing the task. Rising with the sun was in tune to the rhythm of Nature's plan. Being fast a foot with a swift hand served well.

Somewhere Justice was smiling. That wise old farmer knew the score. His favored seedling had landed on fertile ground.

The day ended. I found my way back. Ethel was waiting, more tempting than I can remember. She eyed me with a mischievous grin and asked, "Ready for more?" Somewhere the Judge was smiling. Bulletproof glass would have to wait.

Braided Twine:
A May-December Rendezvous ...

"Mystery and deceit fascinated," Regina thought while taking a side view of her voluptuous body. She learned to use it in having her way with men. No one had thought to ask why games were played: You win and there are times it takes a bazooka to keep on winning.

Her bazooka came in a black spandex girdle. Usually someone got hurt. She longed for the days of innocence when the truth was found in the magic of a twine braided engagement ring and Eli's hard body. We all lose virginity. For her, it happened across a cold slab of stone in a South Bronx cemetery. The soft summer breeze sweetened his wisdom but became the cause for every dim view she had about games men played.

* * *

Regina recounted the tale that had become a favorite story ritual at the Do-It-To-It beauty salon, where most went to either get the low-down or have their reality checked. Hazel the proprietor, Regina's hair processing guru, was also known as the neighborhood shrink. She never tired of listening to Regina's tale; it was good for business. However, there was something sad about chasing fantasies that meant searching but never quite finding.

"Sleep with snakes," Hazel warned, "you become one." Her philosophy was in sorting out answers as easily as she would untangle nappy hair. Gossip reigned supreme at the Do-It-To-It, but today was special. Regina couldn't wait to break the news.

"You're getting married?!" Hazel shouted with her brows leaping to the top of her wired-framed glasses. Eyeing Regina's tight-fitting jeans, she added with a grin, "That lead bucket got you into trouble." Regina wasn't a stranger to strenuous weight training. Her muscled rump could launch a battleship. A gracious, full figure attracted men and one, in particular, who could pass as her son.

"Unload your burden to Mama," Hazel invited. "Just pull up a seat and spare no details." Regina began her tale with what she learned about love and that Eli was her teacher.

"This ring is for always," he said, slipping the twine on her finger, adding how he would replace it with a diamond. Regina never suspected that his 'someday' would be twenty-five years later. So much for promises, she thought, remembering how he didn't bother with a good-bye.

"It has been a long time," he said upon his return, then asked if they could be friends.

"Have you been living in a vacuum? Why didn't you tell me your family was moving out of state—afraid you weren't going to get any?" "I didn't know how to say it," he said.

"You could have tried!" she said, adding, "I missed that dreamer whose idea about dating meant a quick trip to imploding buildings and new-found demolition sites."

That dreamer became an architect and eventually married, he added, revealing the past he promised to share. "Funny, the wife reminded me of you."

"Could anyone be that gullible?" Regina asked.

"She's gone," Eli replied with sadness clouding his eyes. Regina wanted to applaud her for not being foolish. "She went into labor and never recovered," he said, adding how the child soon followed.

"I am sorry," Regina offered, feeling very foolish and wanting to comfort him in some way.

"Who said life was supposed to be fair?" he replied. "All I had left was an architectural degree. But what good is it to me if I don't have anyone to share it with? That's enough about me."

"Well, I don't have an architectural degree." "So, who's the lucky man?" "I never married."

"Why didn't you?"

"I stopped believing in Camelot."

"Regina," he replied with a pathetic pause, "I'm sorry for leaving like I did. However, how long are you going to hold that against me?" "When salmon stop swimming upstream," I answered.

"Regina, we were just kids."

"That's the problem," Regina said. "You took it like a game." "You still hold a grudge?"

"You should have trusted me enough to say goodbye."

"Right, but you know I don't like goodbye," he said, adding, "I'd rather say 'until then' when we start over again."

"What makes you think I would want you?" "Just a thought," he said, cradling my hands. "Well, you are too late!" "Regina, I made a mistake."

"So did I in comparing others to you."

"Perfection exists in one's mind. It isn't real," he argued. "You're right! Dreams were meant for fools."

"Dreams have faults," he said, adding, "and I have mine." I agreed, but it took Jason to set things straight.

"Who's Jason?"

Regina couldn't help smiling. "He plays trumpet in my nephew's band." "Sounds interesting," Hazel replied. "Introduce us."

"Forget it! We're old enough to be his mother!" "That didn't stop you," she said with a chuckle.

"Bedding down with him was the furthest," Regina replied. It all started quietly when we met that night. I had stopped by to offer my nephew a ride after rehearsal, but he had left with the others. Instead, I discovered a musician whose dedication was uncommon for someone with broad shoulders and a strong tight body. I expected his type to be chasing or running from women like me.

"Do you mind if I listen?"

"It's fine with me," he said. "I like sexy women around when I play." May-December? I was flattered he thought of me that way.

"The evening allows lovers to hide in shadows," he said, surprising me with his talent for words. I couldn't help wondering what else he could do. I got lost in the sweet melodies that seemed to reveal my life story from his horn. I kept asking myself, "How old did he say he was?" And then I began making allowances for the difference in our ages. Fifteen years, give or take a few, would have been fine. "Damn! Why wasn't I born earlier?"

"But if love is pure, why hide?" he asked. "Shadows add flavor to forbidden fruit," he said, killing me softly with his song. *Good answer,* I thought, touched by his dedication to music—a quiet honesty that had been missing with Eli.

"I won't kiss and tell," Jason said in offering an unmistakable and bold proposition. But my conscience warned me to be cautious, knowing he and I wouldn't be free without a minor scandal concerning someone 'robbing the cradle'.

However, I wanted to know more about him and not appear obvious. I disguised interest as protection that had me dreaming scenarios with him ending up in my bedroom. I blamed Eli for this. *Why did he leave me?* It was a question that left no answers other than the sound of a ticking clock.

"Hot damn," Hazel exclaimed, reaching for the curlers. "Did Eli and Jason ever meet?"

"Hold on! I'm coming to that," Regina answered. "I dated Eli. He asked to marry me the afternoon they both came calling. I played the perfect hostess, cordial to both. I quietly favored Eli. 'And Jason is a dear friend,' I said, offering a brandy stinger—thinking about the years I'd spend for serving drinks to a minor.

"A friend of Regina," Eli replied, extending his hand and adding, "A man's intentions are judged by the firmness of a handshake." Their grip confirmed their dislike for the other. However, Eli paid Jason the greatest tribute, summed up in two words. "Good grip!" I was impressed with Eli's gesture that had me wondering what more I would have given had Jason not been present. I dismissed those thoughts when Eli left.

"My door is open," I said. I didn't sleep well that night; I kept thinking about my shameless invitation. Eli returned. His touch was strong and firm. It felt safe—secure.

"You deserve more than bedspring serenades," he whispered. All seemed so right. My limbs locked about his narrow waist and drew him in. We had the room rocking with grunting from a four-post bed. The front door slammed against our morning into the night. It had to be Jason. He heard it all! I sought to repair the damage, but Eli began questioning my ties to Jason.

"If you can't trust, leave," I snapped, giving Eli little choice than to assume there was more to my commitment to Jason and that marriage plans would have to wait.

Eli didn't wait long. He was seen entering the side door of the Saint James rectory, where a sassy 'fat ass' accountant resided. Rumors swirled about how she kept men babbling like children for a chance with her.

"I don't care what Eli does," Regina lied when Hazel explained how Eli didn't leave until dawn. "And with all that meat," Hazel added, "it became more surprising he could stand."

How Hazel had found out about the visit never came up. "But I turned him out," Regina lamented. "Why should he commit to me?" Regina resolved the tryst as nothing more than just a one-night stand. Jason was quick to agree! This left more questions as to why he was defending Eli.

Regina continued her story. "The summer months slipped into autumn with no word from Eli. He stayed true to his character: He had left me before. Jason was near; that evening he tore into the flesh of an over-ripe orange. It became unsettling watching him devour the tender meat along with thoughts I had about protecting him."

"Pass the brush," Hazel said with a snap of her fingers; an understanding with a former lover often leads to the bedroom. "Give him credit," Hazel surmised. "Jason was just playing you."

"Probably so, but who was I to throw stones?" Regina admitted. "I was using him. Nevertheless, I hadn't seen Jason for several weeks afterward until returning from the market. He moved quickly to help, but the weight of his good deed soon had his bladder in a vise-like grip. Groceries spilled across the floor. Innocence showed in his scrambling. Ignoring the moment seemed the best remedy. I straightened up with tears streaming my cheeks. Jason slipped on a rolling pin, stating he had been touring the Catskills with a Rock-Band. His stumbling would've drawn a greater crowd. Yet I wanted to believe him. I felt his absence had more to do with Eli.

"Jason had returned despite how I had treated him. 'Do you remember when we met?' I asked, turning the lights down low and then adding, 'I like how you took charge, calling my name.' I sat opposite him in a thick upholstered chair, forever mindful of the length of my short skirt. 'I never forgot what you said about the night allowing strangers to hide in shadows.' A strong brandy sealed the deal."

After forty-five minutes, brandy had Regina baying at the moon. "Why act surprised?" Regina taunted, stripping. "It's what men want, and I'm sure the tradition didn't stop with Eli."

"Not this way," Jason resolved. "Then you'd better be going," Regina snapped. Jason was at a loss. Regina became a bitch in heat, needing some old-fashioned sex. "You'd better be going," she said. Lovely words alone weren't going to satisfy an urge to get even or forget Eli's night with the accountant: It summoned revenge: *Eli got his,* Regina thought, determined to get hers. She found an excuse to keep Jason. She carried out a plan that began with her drawing the curtains, shrouding the room in darkness.

Regina had Hazel locked in as she continued, "I just had fun, good and plenty! I didn't care, and Eli wasn't going to get any! And there was Jason with a chance to play, hoping I'd let him have his way. I could read it in his eyes.

I was in control; pulling the strings and got Jason to grab a handful.

'What's holding you back?' I asked. 'Are you saying you don't want me?' The answer was written on his face.

'Go Home!' I replied to be sure he felt denial's sting. The telephone rang; it wouldn't quit. 'Who's calling me?'

"I brushed against him in answering. The force knuckled his dick against my fleshy rump. He held me, grinding against me! I moved out of his reach. The phone continued ring. He was on my back. . . 'I can't do my Yoga!' I protested, rolling over. Oh crap, I thought. Weren't you going home?

I got rug burns on my ass. Jason got them on his knees! He gaped at my butt encased in sheer pink panties. "You still want to play?" I challenged, stripping my blouse, but I left my bra on, letting him see how the straps cut into my shoulders and back. His nose flared; his nostrils blew steam. I enjoyed thinking about running, knowing he would chase.

I had shattered Jason's Camelot dreams like Eli had broken mine. I gave a smile, but Jason returned it with a glare. He was betrayed. "No more talks about Eli," he said, telling me to shut up and get against the wall!

"Oh no, honey," I answered with mock surprise, "I don't like the tone of your voice." Jason wasn't in a playful mood; his eyes were on fire. "That's no reason to show disrespect."

"Apologize!" I demanded, crazed, offering no mercy. I rejoiced in his pain. It was all so pathetic. I got his hormones jumping, but Eli had my heart though he was humping that accountant. I could imagine him hitting that G-spot—shifting so that his tip causing a burn, making it feel like she's got to piss. That's what I wanted—the way Eli was giving it. Jason was right when he said Eli had made his choice. I needed little urging in determining that my decision was long overdue. I gave in to Jason. . .

He urged me on to my stomach and nudged me on to my knees and stripped my panties. I felt his hands and the heat rushing my body. His lips surrounded my nipple and sucked. I was thinking how good Jason would feel inside my mouth—tasting him and absorbing his scent. I was thinking of how I would make him shiver when I played with his balls. Then I opened my blouse and cupped my breasts. My nipples were hard. I couldn't stop there. I wanted more— fingers caressing me. I begged him not to stop! I wanted it soft. I wanted it hard! I closed my eyes.

Jason's teeth were at my throat. We kissed. His parched lips drew the breath from me. His fingers traced a path to my navel in continuing the symphony— playing me like the pearl tips to his trumpet. He was all up on my back, his dagger sunk into the depths! I lay prone. He inched forward. His blood was pumping; his heart skipped; his breathing came in ragged gasps.

Regina squirmed and writhed. Her legs parted, showing the backs of her thighs and a glimpse of her treasure trove, moist and waiting. The hairs on the backs of her legs seemed to stand on end. Jason slithered into her passion. She contracted with him in a tight, slick but secure fit. She was dripping—the juices trickled along the length of his anatomy. He could feel her nappy hairs scratch and tease with a slight arch of her hips. He held for a moment, feeling spasms rising. He was about to bust a nut. Regina moaned with a soft and sultry whisper, "Give it, baby, don't hold back!" He took her full hips. He draped his body across her back and surged into her, and then slithered to the throbbing of her passion bucking and carrying him home.

They soared then drifted into each other. He gasped and pounded his body between Regina's scissoring limbs! They ascended to catapulting throes of spasmodic contractions, igniting a second volley of exploding crescendos.

"Eli phoned," Regina said. "His words were endearing, but I wanted to slap his face."

"What happened to that donkey butt accountant you spent the night with?" "That was business," he insisted, asking,

"How did you find out?" "There's little this neighborhood doesn't know."

"Then you know Saint James is planning a new wing to the chapel. And my firm will be developing the project."

"How could I have been so blind?" Regina lamented. She lost innocence long since the days of Camelot. All it took was a little trip to her hair salon psychiatrist to realize that she had been holding a grudge against all men because of one. Regina set out to avenge the wrong done some twenty-five years earlier. Jason was just fair game and yet the last person she had wanted to hurt.

I had become the snake Hazel had prophesied. I begged Jason to forgive me for how I used him. He looked on, saying, "Let's be glad for the time we had." He understood; once again, he was a little too forgiving.

"Your friend did visit the accountant," he said.

"What has that got to do with us?" I asked. Jason grinned, showing a flare for being a masterful manipulator, saying how beauticians weren't good at keeping secrets and that there was no end to how an inquiring mind would interpret the truth concerning what men and women did in the shadows at Saint James parish until dawn.

"So, he played me too!" Hazel volunteered, catching on to where all this was leading. "He told me about the meeting, knowing I would tell you."

What he didn't reveal was the source—after reading the parish bulletin searching for musicians to support a fund-raiser—and that Eli would handle the construction project.

I was still a bit confused as to what Hazel was getting at. Hazel smiled, asking, "Don't you get it, girlfriend?" She paused, laughing and admitting, "The boy is too slick for words! He had us all thinking that Eli's visit was to get some B-O-O-O-T-A-A-A-Y!"

There was one more piece to this puzzle that held the scheme together, and that was how Jason suspected I would do almost anything to get back at Eli had I discovered his cheating. I hadn't made a commitment to him, or he to me, which kept us free. Jason arrived on cue. "The pawns were in place," I finally summarized.

"Yes sir, buddy! Jason had better watch his back the next time he passes my shop," Hazel concluded with a quick snap of her fingers, asking, "Have you seen him?"

"I am sure he feels I betrayed him," I answered.

"Time has a way of healing," Hazel said, adding that it was better to leave vengeance with a power greater than time.

I had to find Eli, and when I did, he smiled, placing a ring braided from twine on my finger.

The Wedding March began. All who had meant the most to me were present, but there was no sign of Jason. When the vows were exchanged, a familiar sound resonated in a melodious strain to a September song, penetrating the autumn air that touched my heart through a gleaming silver trumpet. It was Jason! We danced. "I wouldn't have missed this for the world," Jason said.

I would have been disappointed if he had. For a fleeting moment, I wanted to be alone with him. "You were born too early," he admitted. I countered with how he was born late. "Please smile if you don't want to see me cry," I said, recalling a midnight ride into the dawn. It revealed a truth that our affair was something that needed to happen, but now it had to end. He kissed my hand.

"Don't be a stranger," I said, but he didn't answer. He departed, strutting in a proud gangster-lean as if he had won a prize. Some time later, I heard someone exclaiming how the trumpet played such beautiful music. A guest replied, "He left alone, and there was a tear in his eye." I ran after him, but when I got to the front door, he was gone.

Religious Tenets

. . .Madison Avenue fashions affected her depression ...

"Adam wanted more than Eve's apple," the wily streetcorner minister preached, "and that got him kicked out of Eden." The comment drew chuckles from the crowd as the minister added, "I will always toast the big leg sister who retrieved a casserole from the oven's lowest rung and allowed eyes to feast on her glory. Blessed is the girdle that held her!" His steamy decree echoed from the city streets outside the courtroom walls.

The lawyer declared his outrage as the judge slammed his gavel against the lawyer's defense. "It was her, even though she lied!" the lawyer's client cried. "She ran me down and smothered me! I couldn't beat her off with a whip!" "IT WASN'T my fault! YOU RAT!" the luscious lady in question replied. "I wouldn't let you get my cat!"

"But I did!" the defendant shouted. "I was up in that grill until she squeezed my rocks! And you made me nibble and suck!"

"Oh Judge," the teary-eyed victim cried, "I'm the victim!"

"Did she make you squeal?" the prosecuting attorney asked the cowering defendant.

"Judge, she made my toes curl!"

"Did you try to get away or did you just stay humping and pumping that big behind?"

"Judge, she ran a finger up in my ass and told me to settle down fast! She hooked and rocked and told me to feed her more. 'Be extra good,' she said. Judge, it was terrible, just terrible…" the defendant replied with a wink.

"It has been fun," she said, slipping into a fresh pair of black see- through panties. Multi-talon garter straps cut into her great thighs, causing him to rise once more. Her Honor had called before Tyrone reached the chamber door. "See you at eight." Her refreshed appeal set his eyes ablaze.

"Yes, Your Honor," he gasped. Justice drew her garter straps and fumbled with the tension in the snap fasteners. Fleshy thighs billowed over nylon tops and drove the lust-starved officer out of his mind. What they had shared earlier was just an appetizer.

"Poor fellow," she murmured, drawing her soldier to attention and into her bubbling caldron. Hormones raged and the fire consumed.

* * *

Mayor Cassidy Erick Albright had locked his chamber door. He was in conference with his trusted ally, Trina Howard. Her immediate task was to grasp the hem of her skirt and raise it above her hips. She was his lieutenant, the next in line should Albright abandon his throne. Trina pranced in garters while flashing thigh-high nylons encasing her legs, setting off small feet perched in stilettos. She would go to any length to please her boss—giving expert advice to the Saint James restoration project.

"Hold all calls," Mayor Albright ordered. When Miss Howard got busy with Albright's zipper, the staff knew better than interrupt. Howard had been selected from the Mayor's political 'think tank' where the eager and brightest interns would gather. He nurtured her, becoming her mentor. As a result, she rose through those ranks and soon became Albright's Lieutenant. She proved sharp and quite witty; her swivel hips and thick booty didn't hurt.

"Remember your health," his luscious lieutenant warned. The Mayor snorted and grimaced. "Your health," the officer moaned taking the Mayor's full thrust. And then he lay still. Mayor Albright was pronounced dead at the scene. The state of affairs wasn't the only cause for concern. Rumors had his people at odds determining the late Mayor's smile.

"Call Tyrone," the new mayor, the Honorable Trina Howard ordered. *Promotion would be in order,* she thought, *and he will report to me!* The task she had in mind had her drooling. Her thick limbs fluttered. She was at a loss explaining her attraction to the court officer. His honesty and work ethics had something to do with it. Women's fascination with his sturdy build trumped all issue. His fault was in being clumsy. Yet he also had a way of offsetting expectations with just being lucky.

Officer Tyrone Bethune often kept his distance despite the number of times the then young attorney came on to him. Amorous gifts were always returned. Trina dressed conservatively. How resplendent she appeared in a long black robe set off by a white collarless Nehru blouse. Her clothing served a purpose. The dress concealed a gift Nature had given.

Officer Tyrone Bethune remained silent, high and firm, looking past sweet secrets Trina held. Vision played! He couldn't get enough of her scent. He honored his badge. But testosterone bubbled like coffee in a pot. Duty called, but those legs tantalized. He couldn't turn from that sculpted rump. The kettle was about to explode with thoughts about her legs and dimpled knees locked about his waist. Her ass would bounce and shake in supporting his weight, with him pumping like a mad bull. If she took off and ran, then he would chase. A staccato march of black stilettos announced her approach. Trina smiled in greeting. Tyrone acknowledged with a nod.

All seemed casual, but Mayor Howard had been checking out the good Officer for quite some time. She couldn't tell what he wanted her from her— business or pleasure. Could he be that dedicated to service that he would pass her by? Madame Howard often would sit alone in her chambers daydreaming about the officer's kindness and what she would do if she could get him alone. Such thoughts warmed the center of her crotch. She could imagine him cupping her squirming ass. Yes! She had something more personal for Officer Bethune and made it mandatory that he carry out his duties. The soldier marched into the Mayor's office. Muscles vibrated in his walk. Trina did all she could to suppress her excitement but still the juices flowed. She turned toward the window allowing a gracious view of her massive behind.

Upon examining a case load of a new assignment, she asked him to move a heavily upholstered sofa, all the better to scope his muscled ass. For all of his good will, the officer was clumsy. He tripped into her mahogany desk. He lay still. Humor replaced concern when the police officer finally moved. *At least he hasn't broken his neck!* Trina surmised, somewhat relieved. His eyes were closed. Trina gazed. All morals, concepts of fairness and decency fled. Trina unzipped his trousers. A smile curled the corners of her mouth. Nothing mattered except for stroking a remarkable tool that crawled in her quickening fist.

Tyrone writhed in confusion. Stomach muscles tensed. Trina shuddered; instincts guided her in releasing a sensitive and opulent tit. Trina sighed, running hands over the slick gland

and peeling the skin far back to expose the thick flange of the corona. "I never thought a man's business could be attractive," she giggled. "He is handsome," she hummed, brushing back her braided locks. She traced a tongue across Tyrone's pear-shaped knob.

"Yes!" she sighed, tasting his male flavor. She inhaled his masculine leather scent. "Yes!" She said, closing her lips behind the ridge. His meaty stump vanished into her hot, drooling mouth. Trina sucked voraciously, tongue snaking. Saliva gathered around his thick tusk. She savored the sensation of closing her teeth behind the firm rubbery ridge that stretched into her throat. She slurped, pressing her chin into him to get more into her gullet.

Fascination abounded in a wild song growing louder. Need pervaded. Her stomach tightened. Hips weaved and shivered in a tempestuous frenzy. But she withdrew from his balls and slipped the robe from her shoulders only to return and encircle him with her gentle fingers. It would be heaven if he would devour her, she thought. If she could gobble his fabulous root, couldn't he return the favor? Trina glanced at his emotion pinched face. "Would you feel like doing it to me?" she asked, licking his tasty oil into her hungry mouth, stifling involuntary contractions brought on by his stretch into her gullet. Tyrone's eyes fluttered. Timid fingers mauled her hot, hard nipples. It challenged bold instincts. She let the bulb slip from her mouth. She gripped his shaft. But the desire to be stuffed became unbearable.

"Yes," Trina sobbed, eyes riveted to his crotch, "I want it in me," she said, coiling about his waist and drawing him on top. She shoved a hand between their bodies and pushed against the resilient head. The python slithered along the crack of her ass. "Yes, my darling, I want you so much."

Trina arched backward and against an oak's gnarled bark. She reared like a mare in heat. Her jockey took control. Sweat glistened from well-muscled haunches. She arched, almost dislodging him. Yet he held tight and surged much deeper to satisfy a delicious ride. Orgasms rushed in breath-snorting pleasure. Yet far too soon she looked on in disdain. The riding warrior lay beaten—groveling at her feet. She stepped across a well-muscled body and adjusted her skirt with disappointment. Still determined to crack that nut, she spread her buns and clapped about his throbbing pole, inching it once more into her fold. "Faster!" Trina implored, arching to his spear. She moaned. "Make it swell! Shove it hard!" Trina shivered to his writhing and slithering thrust. He slapped her ass. Passion exploded and then overflowed. Orgasms ripped in a violent surge. The learned woman writhed in a chaotic entangle of scissoring limbs. They cried and sighed. Tyrone lay draped across his Mistress' thick, quivering rump.

Officer Tyrone Bethune stood at attention when the Mayor's motorcade passed the courthouse. A smile drifted across Trina's lips remembering a leather upholstered sofa that had to be moved to the other side of her office. When events of the day were settled, she placed an urgent call for Tyrone … after all, another sofa had to be moved.

The Awakening: The trophy

It was a Saturday afternoon down at the corner barbershop. The men got horny just talking about the size of Greta Williams' booty, including Jasper, her ex-boyfriend who couldn't be trusted. He lied about everything. No one at the shop believed him when he bragged about how he rode that large, well-shaped ass. *How large?* they questioned "You had to see it find it," he replied. He described how her rejection left him throbbing with a dull case of blue balls. "Oh, the pain!" he moaned. Passion rushed his groins. The lusty Amazon continued to tease with her girdled ass. He was just shot down. It didn't help bathing her with kind wishes that placed his nose deep in her cleavage. He walked away a broken man but plotted his next move: "I won't bother you anymore," he replied. "I know the deal! Those tits aren't real!"

"WHAT! FOOL! Didn't they teach you anything at school?" The lady grabbed him by the back of the head and had him thinking about finding another plan. She took him into another room and yanked her blouse, exposing her bulging chocolate orbs: "Give them a kiss!" He grabbed two handfuls of her voluptuous ass cheeks to keep his balance. He buried his face between the twin pillows. . . And so, my hero continued his romping adventure behind the closed door, where the sound of a belt buckle coming undone and a zipper unzipped echoed throughout the apartment. The outcome became apparent where his pinnacle was planted. My adventure remained a plan just in bloom.

And that plan was to steal Shannon's panties. She had a large behind. I just wanted to know how big. She caught me stealing her panties from the clothesline. It had been my plan to take those secrets and quiet the night when I lie awake thinking about her. My knees buckled thinking about her. I couldn't stand it. So fluffy the dream! She was tall and thick. But she insisted that I had better 'get lost' or she would make me wish I had. She would've crushed me! Yet that little bit of action had me dreaming of back breaking shift supervisor at a food packing plant. I was looking for work. This was just an interview, or so I thought.

I entered the apartment and sat back with ease, not letting on how molten fever rushed in my veins. For this was the second time I had ever been alone with her, not yet able to forget about the first. The quietness, the solitude surged through my veins with passion. I wasn't going to let on how much she stirred something inside of me. We engaged in some small talk and then things got shaky when she started teasing about my trying to steal her panties. I admitted that it was just a foolish thing to do. "And what were you planning to do with them?" she asked. I stumbled for answers. I had been transported back to a time when an awkward youth realized the beauty of a mature, full-figured woman. Miss Shannon said she would have given me her girdle had I asked. I didn't know it then, but maybe she was just playing me to see how far I would lean. She sat opposite me, allowing a view of her big legs. Shannon crossed the floor to play a few tunes and let the summer evening breeze weave its magic. That night went really well. Few words were spoken.

She reminded I was much older than the day we first met. She thought I was cute. Shannon straddled my lap. Her fingers were busy at my belt buckle. My zipper became undone. I was free but for the moment when she engulfed me. The comforting heat of her hot breath became an inferno. She slid back, crossed over and then down. "So, this is where that good dick has been hiding." I was trapped between her fleshy thighs with my nut sack slapping on her rump. She gave me fits, making me suck that sweet kitty. Her cries summoned the storm! She squealed like Aunt Myrtle when Uncle Fred mounted that booty. I waited for years to pass when with glee it was time for me and Jezebel's daughter. I humped—just pumping and jumping all up in that grill. I lingered there when she ran a finger up in my ass and told me to push harder! She hooked my hole and told me to feed her hard pole! I recaptured my breath and humped and pumped away. She rolled onto her back and drew me between her flailing limbs, whipping me alongside the head and warning about being extra good with her kitty! We fucked, squeezed and teased, grinding hard and doing it slow, not just for style—I was too damned tired. "What a dirty trick!" She grunted and rolled; I grooved her deep dark crevice. "I need more dick!" she said, slipping into her panties and making for the door. The thought she was leaving and soon would be giving it to someone else—there was no telling what or whom she would be doing when left to prowl with no limits. I ached with jealousy that it wouldn't be me. The thought of losing the best chance I've had sapped strength; depression settled. Many scenarios rushed my mind. Visions of someone getting that booty increased my urgency. He would be riding that high sloping ass—so high that his knees would touch the mattress. That sorry bastard couldn't handle it. Her bucking and shivering would drain a strong man senseless. Yet I'd give my left nut to take his place! But wait! She hadn't left yet! My last chance! She was encased in stretched panties that shielded her swollen pussy. One more try! I must not fail.

"Who's there?" she moaned, feeling her lover's tongue darting in her back door. "Just call it the hole, my daring stranger." Shannon was out of her mind with joy, but she continued to protest. "Stop it!" Her legs open wider. "Greedy eyes see, but you get no ride! And I am not going to be your holster! Oh, merciful me," she continued in feigned sorrow. I mounted and plunged to the hilt. "I'm wide open!" she declared. I speared, feeling her walls tickle and caress my shaft. I withdrew and then sent it flying. She tightened around me and milked so that I throbbed and convulsed in waves of orgasmic ecstasy.

The years shed away like the peeling of an onion. I encountered Shannon's conversation that inspired the timid to sprout words of wisdom if it meant he would be getting her panties. Then as now her fragrance aroused the passion in me. I took the opportunity, noticing how her butt protruded with a perfect overhang shading the back of her thighs. I pressed and grooved in her dark crevice. "Greedy eyes see! Greedy teeth grit! None of this you will get!" she said, explaining she was lying on a beach towel trying to catch some sun before her husband arrived.

"What are you looking, at fool?" she said, grinding her hips to a more comfortable resting spot. I had stumbled upon her quiet and most personal moment. I was sure to get an invite had I played innocent, but I couldn't stop drooling. She spread the blanket. With a cruel grin, she smiled, saying, "Stare all you want but you aren't getting any!" Yet she teased with a swayback lean on hands and knees, arching her thick rump just a little bit higher. Fire! Desire! "Let me," I begged.

"You still aren't getting any!" she declared. "You're too young and you'd probably fill my bucket before I was ready to cum." At least she was thinking about it when she said 'probably.' I wanted her so bad! I was near tears. Shannon continued the pose, flashing that big fleshy ass with cellulite dimples, spiking the blood to rush my veins. My head throbbed. I maintained; my jock absorbed the awful strain. But there she lay with face down, ass high, ignoring me. I was nothing more than a hapless eunuch. She gazed over her shoulder to dare me. If this was a test, then I was failing. I couldn't help feeling what she needed was more than a good fuck!

I buried myself in her thick ass! She quivered and jumped every time my nose nudged her puckered hole. "All up in the rump," she yelled. "Lick it, you nasty bastard!" I attacked with a greedy, slobbering tongue! Lust stole her resolve. She opened wide, all the while moaning. I was in her with a thick dick where I became the destroyer. I pinched, bit her clit and drove into another fit. She rose once more on hands and knees, face down, ass high and sopping wet. She felt me behind her. She ground into me, all the while moaning and reaching to caress my nut sack slapping her fat rump. I held firm to keep my place! Sweet pleasure gushed and flowed until she collapsed and begged me to stop! "He's arriving soon!"

"Let me find that spot," I said, continuing jacked-up urgency. She was on her back and letting me into her fit. I busted a nut; she squealed and kicked. Her fat legs slammed, driving me deeper. She slapped, spanked and caressed. Flashing lights! I came again in an upward roll across her big fleshy booty in a final and pleasurable gallop. I lost all sense of time. She shifted onto her back.

"What about your husband?" I asked. "I'll never tell if you won't," she replied, trembling and shivering. I took her limbs over my shoulders and pushed so that her thighs were against her breasts with her feet snug at my armpit. That gash was hot and flushed; I continued in the delicious flow!

"Please," she said as I pressed harder, spilling her breasts across her chest and at her armpits. She appeared sedated, belabored breathing? "How long have you waited?" No time for calling the power. I was throbbing and grabbing in a delirious state of mind. My one-eyed willy was on target ... I just wanted to buckle her knees and stuff that roaster! Her eyes rolled to the top of her head. Tremble! Gasp! Explode! Her scent wafted throughout and mixed with the sultry air, igniting a sweet and throbbing release. The seduction was complete, with pushing and pulling in a touching embrace. Sweat dripped as she curled her toes in an orgasmic fit erupting and claiming souls of those who sought to listen. Lightheaded, tired, wired, and on a limb, she asked, "Did you get what you've been missing?"

Sweet Meat

. . . And then there were women proud of what she possessed . . .

Gig Gail was quite aware how extra poundage strategically placed complemented her roommates' more passionate appeal. The two were used to parading in their panties to combat the heat in their small studio on sultry summer evenings. "Men can't cope with all this meat!" Gail said, teasing and admitting how her roommate's voluptuousness was turning her on. "If I had my way I would lick, suck and nibble until you started farting in tongues. I would grind you until your bones quaked with your stomach on fire and your brain bursting in multiple orgasms." Gail was high—quite confident. She licked her lips and then burst into laughter. "I would have you gushing like a torrential tsunami," she said. "And when you think, I am going to let you release, I'll have you face down, begging for a strap-on slapping at your ass in each pounding push. By the time I let you release you'd be crying like a baby, gasping and grabbing, pushing me back to make me stop. And when I get back to sucking, you're going to burn your zip code so that your man will never find you."

Thick horny women and a bottle of sweet wine on a sultry night behind closed doors raised possibilities. Nothing like a man who can rise above the challenge, Gail would often reply. And yet with contradiction she maintained, "They just can't be trusted!"

"Then why do you play?" Lori, Gail's roommate, replied. Gail shook her head in disbelief, realizing her friend had a lot to learn. "Grow up girl! Because I don't trust doesn't mean I don't want a little bit every now and then!" Gail said to enter a local lingerie boutique. "Men are ready to strap a saddle!"

Lori couldn't suppress laughter, recalling an old song lyric that matched her friend's psyche. "First you say you do and then you don't! Then you say you will and then you won't!" Rumors had it that the boutique store manager held the key to Gail's desire, a pair of diaphanous panties if she would model for him. That day Gail returned with a dozen pair. She maintained that all men wanted one thing. Still, Lori kept options open. She had a thoughtful friend, Jake, whistling like the rest. He wanted that ass. Getting with Lori wasn't a secret. The more Jake tried; the more Lori ignored. The more Lori ignored, the more she turned him on.

"Oh my!" she replied when he told how he appreciated her size. Lori only smiled in remembering a health food magazine describing women her size being obese. "There's nothing overweight about those curves," Jake replied, inviting her into the backseat of an old Ford pickup. She laughed when he asked about her pendulous orbs. "Will you take care of my friends?" she asked, stretching her arms above her head. "I won't neglect your twins!" Jake answered with pinching fingers across her firm thighs.

Lori had been shopping when Jake saw her. She appeared worn, with the need to rest, and so he did the routine gentlemanly thing, offering to take her home. She accepted. Fate must have been smiling. Fatigue was gone. Lori sat quite composed. Jake seized the opportunity, inching across her thighs. She squirmed. It was just the van, but all seemed right behind tinted windows. They wrestled until her foot hooked under his armpit. Bulging limbs shot over his shoulder.

"You're fast," Lori murmured, hard and cumbersome. Her breasts swelled, ready to explode. "Won't you let me see them?" he asked, nuzzling the hollow of her throat. "Do you have condoms?" she asked, unhooking her bra. "What has that got to do with my eyesight?" Her breasts sprang forth. Jake pinched and pulled two hands full. "Not so hard!" she grimaced.

"Stop!" Lori snapped yet writhed impatiently. Her passionate invitation was irresistible. He struggled with her panties. His zipper got twisted. Windows grew steamy. Sweat pooled; he ripped at his crotch to free himself. Jake plunged into Lori; she raised her hips and thighs to engulf his him deeper into her twitching core. His shaft touched bottom; she grasped his ass cheeks and let out a howl of delight.

"O-o-o-o, Jake!"

Jake hoisted Lori's thighs over his shoulders. She rocked her hips allowing him clear passage. "Oh Jake," Lori sighed to the passion exploding inside of her. Ecstasy filled the intimate quarters of the backseat. Lori jerked her beautiful head from side to side. She was cumming and so was he. Some time later, cradling him against her breast, she said, "You just need a little help." Together they tripped into Dante's inferno, wallowing and Jake swallowing rock hard nipples. Friction burned in storm's fury. Lori grunted. The van rolled. Traffic stood still in horn-blasting unison. Miles and Dizzy played with an assist from Coltrane. It was one hell of a jam.

Angelina Harding:

. . . She had a big ole butt . . .

Before Reverend Harding's death, the sultry Angelina Harding had worn black. Large dark glasses hid secrets. Rarely did she smile.

After Reverend Harding's death, she assumed the patriarchal chair, the spiritual leader. The transition of authority was smooth and flawless. The new pastor craved her support, but like most men, he gave in to a coke-bottle waistline and a voluptuous body that made floorboards squeak. Few remained unscathed by the grinding gyrating beneath her skirt. Men found a cause to rush her bedroom in a self-serving attempt to ease her suffering. The knowledgeable Angelina turned them away and recalled her husband's work that had to be completed. She became the stone upon which the congregation stood.

Though now in my forties I couldn't forget the images of my youth. I was nineteen when Angelina organized the third pilgrimage to the South Carolina Christian Conference. She gave orders like a field marshal settling an army that had been rushing like marbles in a pinball machine. She ushered the congregation aboard the Greyhound bound for Charleston. I settled back and soon drifted off with visions contending with James Crow laws and the Southern Confederacy. Even the children thought it wise for blacks to travel in groups when dabbling with Southern hospitality. We'd stop where large clapboard outhouses stood to wait.

I was young enough for my aunt to take me with her, either because I wouldn't know what I was looking for or wouldn't know what when I found it. In the company of women old enough to be my mother, I wouldn't dare, or even care to look. However, my aunt read the excitement in my eyes when the other buses arrived, and others filed out. All I wanted was to take a grip and park myself behind a knothole outhouse wall. What I saw made my temperature rise. The choir director was sopping wet. A member of another church appeared quite concerned about all that groaning commotion. The stranger waited until all the occupants had left and then went to investigate.

"Sister, is there something I can do?" The choirmaster turned in haste and forgot to rearrange a skirt that remained bunched around her waist. The aide stepped and planted himself between the choirmaster's awesome cheeks. He took her fast. The choirmaster's eyes rolled and blinked. I thought she would call for help, but instead she held to keep from falling into the commode. The stranger plunged like sumo wrestlers trying to get at the last pan of smothered chicken. I didn't know what to make of the scene because the stranger wore a dress and a skewed wig. It looked like a lot of fun, and I wanted 'in', but was ignored. When it was over, the stranger was never seen again. The choirmaster sat all throughout the trip.

"You are young, but not as young as I thought," my aunt said, snapping me back from a stolen memory. She ordered me to wait outside the commode. Again, I got lucky when discovering another knothole.

Skirts were drawn. Garters were adjusted about pairs of massive, crushing thighs. Angelina stood among the flock in a spandex girdle. Her summer skirt swirled about, showing faint impressions of the multi-talon garter straps about her luscious broad hips. She watched me out the corner of her eye yet pretended I wasn't there. She stepped outside, eyeing the bulge in my jeans. "How old did you say you were?" she asked with a knowing look. I didn't say; in fact, it was the first time she had ever spoken to me. She clipped my chin and returned to the flock.

The trip didn't finish without issues. Motel Bungalows, where we stayed, needed plumbing, but it didn't explain why an electrician, a short man, was entering Angelina's apartment. I guess she was the first in line? Whimpering cries followed. I ventured to investigate. The phantom electrician returned the following night. "Jed! I didn't expect you back so soon," Angelina said, locking the door, but in truth she was waiting—hoping. She grew more impatient. She didn't like waiting. When he arrived, she didn't wait for his alibis. She hiked her billowing skirt. "You like what you see?" she snapped. "And then what took you so long? "Is that your screwdriver or are you just glad to see me?" Angelina teased extending her arm to his well, well-padded crotch. "Angelina, you haven't changed!" he gasped.

"We've got some catching up to do," Angelina replied. Jed owned the complex but adding Angelina to his domain was like trying to catch snowflakes in a frying pan. She had become obsessed; I didn't recognize her. Jed drew nearer. "Don't just stand there like you don't know what I'm talking about," Angelina said, glancing over her shoulder in offering her broad behind. "You remember too, don't you?" Jed couldn't forget a quiet field trip with her.

"You remember? Don't play that surprised look," she taunted. "OH LORD!

NO BABY! NOT HERE! LET'S GET INTO bed!" However, the 'let's' was not fast enough.

"You're NASTY!" Angelina snapped when Jed shouted how he wanted to get in her ass. Yet his need inspired her to spread just for him! "You're shameful," she scolded, greasing her hole through her diaphanous panties. "Don't you ever get enough?" Angelina giggled. She was now flushed and gushing, fooling no one for she was just as anxious. "You bastard!" Jed had her face down with her ass bouncing high!

He would have been a better lover had he kept his glasses. Angelina leaned and pushed him across the bed. He fell with an awful thud, hitting his head. He lay still. Amanda showed no mercy, straddling his face and plastering his mouth shut. Eyes bucked and blinked. She rode his face and wouldn't let go until she blasted another. "I can't breathe!" he mumbled. Angelina laughed, thinking back to how he had grabbed her hips and mumbled into her crotch. She had no idea that she was smothering him.

Orgasms ripped, sending violent tremors through her thick, voluptuous body. "I said no chewing allowed," she murmured; Jed slurped, working it to the core. Angelina was ready for him and enabled a glide that missed the mark. He plunged her tight ribbed canal, the winking backdoor. A second volley burst with him well embedded. "You devil!" she grunted. Jed fell and slithered deep and emptied himself in a long pulsating flow. Angelina shook and protested yet quivered to his impetuous throb. She burst and streamed.

Five years had passed since I had joined the pilgrimage. I hoped to regain faith that had been replaced by slot machines and games of chance. If asked, I couldn't deny that my return to the Church had everything to do with Angelina's black garter strap fasteners and gossamer nylons.

A humid Sunday morning during Bible study made one aware of the old saying about a hard dick having no conscience. Tight skirts and Egyptian musk taunted. Angelina clutched her Bible and preached. Although what she said had value, the message got lost in familiar stirrings that gathered at my crotch. Her skirt inched higher, allowing a view of gleaming garter straps eating into her fleshy thighs. "What you're looking at, Mister?" She walked toward me. Blood raced through my veins, expecting a righteous backhand. A smile curled the corners of her mouth. The 'WORD' wasn't all that held my attention.

Once more, I found myself among the flock. The pilgrimage was in session, but again sleeping quarters were scarce when we arrived. Someone screwed up the reservations. Angelina offered to share her room with me—I could bunk down on a spare cot, she said. When alone, the God-fearing matron laughed, recalling how she once caught me eyeing her from a knothole in the old roadside outhouse.

I wondered would she have been so quick in sharing her room had she known I had seen her giving it up to Jed. She said she admired those who could keep a secret and how doing that went a long way in earning her respect. I didn't know where this conversation was leading, but I didn't have to wait long. She knew I had witnessed her play with Jed. Her tone changed with a sudden chill in the evening breeze.

All doubts were confirmed when she said it wasn't very nice spying on her! Although she frowned, I couldn't help feeling that she enjoyed the idea that young men were still talking about her. I promised not to tell. "Refer to me as Angelina." She reclined on a large bed. "Just knock before entering," she said.

Angelina wasn't home when I returned. Somewhat disappointed, I drifted off to sleep but was awakened by the sound of a steady stream from the bathroom. The woman was on the commode with a half-slip, griping. Panties settled at her ankles. Her fingers disappeared into a thick patch of tight curls, inflaming passion like gasoline to the fire.

What fantasies must have been running through her brain? Did it have something to do with her plumber? Her stroking fingers increased in speed. Her thighs flew open with a flutter. She hissed and whimpered.

"Is there something I could do to help?" I asked, pretending to ignore the passion. "And how do you propose to help, my darling?" she asked with a mischievous smile. She crossed the room with her clinging half-slip sculpting her massive hips and grinding buttocks in full display. She unhooked her bra.

I was about to explode. Angelina laughed when she saw the state, I was in. "You need a little assistance," she teased, calling me into her room. "You're just right for the oven," she murmured then asked whether I liked what she was showing me. The room seemed smaller. The walls were closing in.

Egyptian musk prevailed with the sight of the silken fabric caressing her luscious thighs. I acted like a mule had kicked me in the groin. "Serves you right for spying on me," she said, cupping me with calm, soothing fingers. She said that in my favor, I never told and that such loyalty needed to be rewarded.

"A mature woman isn't a toy," Angelina said caressing me and massaging the ache that was driving me out of my mind. She drew her slip across her thighs. I stood transfixed at the bulging crotch of her panties. I cupped her, feeling her fullness. She stepped toward me, grinding against the bulge in my trousers. I moved my hands so that I reached her thick rump. It was exciting stroking and spanking a full and thick panty-encased rump. I sought her deep, dark crevice. And then with fingers poised, I inched into her brown eye. She unzipped and caressed. Cold fingers soothed before feeding them into her hot mouth.

Her hands wandered across my thigh. The sudden shock buckled my knees. I slipped to the floor and joined her, face-to-face and kneeling. I encircled her waist and let my hand come to rest on the upper slope of her large behind. I traveled to the hem of her skirt, gathering it above her hips. I removed her bra and fed her breasts into my mouth; I weighed the fullness of each. Our lips met in a tongue- slithering frenzy. It was good how we swayed against each other. Her hands were on me and clawing. She pulled me on top of her full- figured frame and opened her limbs, allowing me to rest against her swollen mound; more kisses and idle words. I urged her on to her stomach. I wanted that large, muscled ass. I mounted her broad behind still with her panties intact until slipping them to the back of her thighs. It awakened the crazed animal inside of me. I clung to her; what more could I do? She knew. 'Have mercy!' Don't chew!" I approached in a trance, yet with each move calculated and gasping. She was hot—such a sensitive spot! "I'll guide you," Angelina whispered. "I want to feel your tongue … Don't stop until I tell you!" One could hear the electricity rushing through the fixtures in the dead silence that cloaked the room. Little movement; no sound? And then the storm; she gasped, kicked and drew me closer. I didn't answer but bit instead. She screamed. "Mercy! It hurts!" Had I gone too far, perhaps not far enough? I wouldn't let her slip from my grip. She swept through my body. Her eyes went into a dazed glare. "Don't worry about your hat! You can stay," she said. "Just keep doing … and stay steady on my… WAAAAAAAAAAAH!" Angelina's screams keyed a ferocious surge. "HAVE MERCY! Bastard! You sweet bastard!" I needn't answer. I wouldn't know what to say even if Shakespeare was straddling the headboard. She was half dead and drained. She looked up from where she lay and mumbled, "I'm going to get you back!"

She shook her fist in my face and said, "Round two is coming— hope your mama paid your insurance!"

"Poor child," she whispered, drawing me closer. "There must be something I can do to ease your suffering, or the suffering you're going to have," she said. It didn't take long to find out what she meant when her fleshy thighs splayed, showing a hairy grotto. "Can you keep a secret?" she asked, reaching from the shadows. Her breast swelled with nipples extending. I trailed a path to her portal. She heaved and encircled me between flailing limbs that were climbing, pounding and just tearing at my ass. Now impaled, her petals fanned feathery touches along my shaft. The action was sweet. The intensity grew. Shivers raced with visions of her with Jed. I should have been jealous and turned her out. But what I was feeling wasn't about jealousy. I just didn't give a damn.

"Stick it!" she cried. Time stood still and quickly lost its meaning. I climbed her massive body and slithered into her mossy portal. She rubbed her crack and pinched. Her ass quivered, bubbled and popped. A man caught watching had no other recourse than to beat that meat to drive his lust into retreat. She cradled. I surged in liquid fire and rocked with a soul splitting frenzy. Tongues swirled and rose with short pummeling strokes. The damn burst into a second volley of convulsive fits.

Sunrise! But it wasn't the only thing rising. I watched the conservative Angelina fasten her stockings. It was time to meet with the congregation but up went her skirt, presenting a massive behind. The traditional Angelina was insatiable. Perhaps that's why she favored dark glasses? She drew her panties up, showing the back of her full thighs to the inviting crevice of her massive hillocks.

I wanted the rest. But Angelina wasn't having any of that! She grabbed and led me to the sofa. She straddled the arm and invited me to slap her behind to red crimson. She bounced and jumped, bathing my length with gushing cream.

"The congregation is going to know you're not just resting," I said. "They're going to know we're getting it on. And that I got your ass cheeks clapping and ready," I declared.

"Who's going to tell?" she asked with a menacing glance. Then she laughed, saying she was going to find a real good plumber. I leaped to burst that gusher. Oozing cream cascaded. Cries escaped the locked door. I left blazing red palm welts.

Angelina wore black with dark glasses. We attended the revival meeting. She squirmed upon needles. She sat but smiled when I passed by and brushed against her. "Don't let your eyes get bigger than what you can handle," she warned. I didn't know where she was going with this. It proved to be wiser to accept the gift and ask no questions when her skirt inched across her luscious thighs. Pastels flashed in the bright light but when darkness settled upon the congregation, lovers hid in the shadows.

Savannah Blaze

Rembrandt, Ruben, and Picasso honored her …

Short billowing skirts didn't hide that fleshy gift shadowing the backs of her upper thighs. Savanna had every man looking. She knew how to strut and finish a glide with a high kick stride.

She'd bust nuts with a heartfelt grind when her lover's hand drifted. She loomed when straightening a nylon seam. She wouldn't let compliments go to her head. Yet speaking from the heart, saying the right words, one might get to sample her sweet mercy. But Savanna was choosy—hard to please and wouldn't just share with just anyone. Her character wouldn't give in to the right looks or fancy words. She would sooner bed down with a hardworking man than one flaunting a fat wallet.

Temp, the building custodian, stepped forward. His words were tight and somewhat harsh. Yet his honesty showed in his drenched shirt and the bulge below his belt loop. Savanna kept stepping to the custodian's music that ended in the back seat of a late old Plymouth van. Passion had gotten the better of him. "But Savanna, I haven't had my fill of your fine behind yet!" This was a real line. He was begging and she liked it. "Tell me how fine," she said with a smile, "and how you are about to go blind looking at my big behind!" Temp was warm and Savanna was getting turned on with his dirty talk. The janitor grinned, saying, "BABY, you're like a pan of hot buttermilk biscuits and a bubbling bowl of beef stew!"

"I'm pleased you think of me like that, but will you take your nose out of my ass?" Before Savanna knew, he was riding her booty. And before long her legs flew across his broad shoulders. Without much grace, she was on her back with limbs locked about his waist. There it is! Don't say you didn't know. It felt so good; he held her broad hips with little urging for her to move. She squirmed, shimmied and shook; her magnificent rump quivered with a slight arch to each twisting thrust. He melted into her fleshy rump.

Savanna presented quite a different story at Sunday morning services. No one doubted her Faith. She would be quick to slap a lasting gleam from an unsuspecting eye. Her glance held my attention. I had seen her with the custodian. And played with telling what I had seen. But she responded, "No one would believe you anyway. And besides, loose lips sink ships," she said with a wink. What I wanted wasn't meant for kids. I couldn't help feeling that she knew what I wanted but didn't have the courage to ask. Yet we were bounded by what was to become our secret. Perhaps, or so I had hoped, she'd find her way to have mercy on me. But the streetwise Savanna from the 'cornbread belt' told me to hang onto Mama's apron strings—that I wasn't quite ready for the frying pan.

Savanna wasn't about just needing a tackle. I lay gasping, weak and limp across her broad rump, rushing to drive her into an orgasmic fit! My eyes were too big for my stomach. There was one way to settle the bursting urge. Let instincts guide to shifting her skirt and watch her kick! I envied the lucky one between her fat thighs and gorging himself at her tits. I envied the man's strain, blessed with age and nature's gift, flinching, plunging, driving him deep between those fleshy hillocks taunting me, the precocious youth. I became the custodian spewing seed—grappling with Savanna.

Savanna Blaze scolded all who doubted the power of Faith. But what she did behind closed doors was her business. I learned not to trust women wearing eyeglasses. Church deacons meant to speak with her. But their zippers got stuck and burst into Dante's inferno. The minister belabored; cream oozed along Savanna's brown thigh and turned dark from nylon's chafe. She cried from the sanctified corridors, "Give it to me, baby! Stick it!"

No questioning or wondering why he was in that twitching and puckering brown eye. I should not have been watching. I thought I would die! I got on my knees and began to pray. But she arched high enough and into her he did fly.

Is it a dream or a convoluted vision? Students searching for Divinity found it in a misery that had risen! Sam throbbed. He got a tub of lard and hobbled into the yard. He hid beneath a bush! It was wrong, but he stroked hard and long. He heard her song: "Why are you hiding when I got this to share?" Savanna proved lewd and crude. The student trembled with fright although he was past twenty-one. Adults had the right to consent. That saying grace kept her from being locked up. I couldn't help feeling betrayal's pain. Had I a whip I would have cut her, smothering her latest fling. Instead, her grinding taunted throughout the night. Visions rushed and abandoned me in wonder. That ass can't be real. But in a beckoning tone she proclaimed, "It's swollen!" she said, "It needs a pin to let out the air!" Was she referring to me? Was she watching me all the time I was watching her? "Make a choice. Come out from under that shrub."

"You're nothing more than an aberration—a freakish thought with an occasion to rise," I moaned. "Why are you teasing me?" I was fooling myself thinking I could just pass her by and escape her rage. I became captive to a dream where all became solid and real. I could see and touch her thick bush nestled between her massive thighs. It weakened me with passion meant for man's pleasure, the kind meant for the mature who could handle it. I couldn't breathe, I was all dizzy in the head—my heart was pounding; it was about to burst. "You're thick!" I said.

"Yes, it's thick," she replied. "Why act surprised? You've seen it before." She knew all along, but I still couldn't believe. My mind wouldn't conceive! "I own your soul," she said, cradling me in an awful grip.

"Lord! Why do you test me?" But the Lord didn't seem to be listening. I couldn't stand it anymore. I begged for release. "Shut up!" she snapped. The release would have to wait. I struggled against what fantasies had brought. I held against the strain, but my body was in pain. I needed her. The bargain was struck. I became the pigeon about to be had. I will roast in Hell. I looked to escape, but Savanna had locked the door. Her dark piercing eyes reached into the soul of me.

"You got me! What are you going to do with me?" She eyed me as if about to change her mind. A cruel smile curled the corner of her mouth. "Are you the one that runs with wolves? Do you get excited when I look at you?" She was sexy and would have made a statue jump. Yeah, I took it all in. She was in control. However, thoughts about being a gentleman became an illusion. I struggled with getting her tight skirt to her hips but succeeded in drawing it to her thighs. I sank my teeth into her throat and pushed her against the wall. She flashed her puckered brown round! Electric shocks went from my head to my jock! She watched me with an amused smile. Somewhere in the back of my mind she was passing judgment. But I didn't care. I wanted her so much that all my inhibitions faded and all that stood between us was the fabric of her diaphanous panties. Thick cheeks clapped as I inched into her with a slight dip of my knees and an upward surge that had her bending on her belly across an old oak table.

Savanna contracted and moved into my lap; I stretched her spastic grotto. It was a perfect fit. BUT OH! Ever So SLOW! I was deep into her, totally engulfed. Hot lava oozed. I pounded and pumped, gritting my teeth to hold back. Pleasure became my enemy, drawing passion from the core of my loins, where spasms twitched and made liars out of players who boast of their conquests. Her full-figured body and slick, tight fit had me counting backward with a resolve not to cum first. I was determined not to leave her hanging. Yet the more I held, the closer I came to the inevitable. It was all good—in fact, just a little too damn good. I needed a sign that meant I didn't have long to wait—that she was near. She trembled and wept, "It's slapping my ass!" Was she ready to blow? She quivered and shook her massive body, arching to meet my surge. Seizures struck with mother earth shifting beneath me. "OH LAWD NO!" Savanna cried. "I can't take any more!" Scarlet ribbons exploded in my head. Orgasms burst in the wake of pulsating spasms that triggered a soul-splitting orgasmic fit. I slipped into a trance where pleasure rained and everything went black!

Savanna awakened saying she had no idea how I could have lasted so long —that she wanted me to cum first. I was more amazed and quite confused as to the part I played in orchestrating this scene where I ended in her bed. I replied that I now know why the custodian may have been limping.

"How old did you say you were?" she asked. I wasn't going to tell. We cuddled well into the dawn. And when the urge hit, she rolled and pulled me on top and between her flailing thighs. Thick legs rose up and then curled across my waist. The strength in her limbs broke my back. She gyrated with upward thrusts to my downward surge into her sweltering nest. She kicked my ass while squealing and grunting to her heavy limbs slamming and locking about my waist. Orgasms burst into sweet oblivion; we floated to earth in a collage of fluttering lace ribbons…

Steamy Curtains …

Virgil the poet applauded …

The kept men scheming and young boys dreaming. She was obsession spiked with hip-grinding passion in a tight skirt. Sultry foreplay to a sweet jazz soliloquy played behind a locked bedroom door. "Do you like it, Sugar?" she asked in a slow, hot whisper. The answer lay tucked in her silk purse where love flowed and then exploded in an infinite passage of inane adjectives and flashing lights. . . 'Baby Got Back.'

She paraded the avenue with her head held high, surveying all through long sweeping eyelashes. Her intoxicating fragrance stirred fantasies. But I was best described as being too old for girls and too young for women. I could watch, but it couldn't stop my dreaming. All had been a foolish game resulting from an overactive imagination and a locked door. Visions of her standing in a waist-clinching corset with dangling garter straps slapping at her lush thighs teased to no end. I had been watching her since an admirer bribed me into delivering a rose bouquet to her apartment.

Fate was kind, for we lived in the same building. That gave me the chance to beg to run her errands. She often stopped for a quick hello. Her nylon-sheathed limbs 'hissed'. She towered over me; she shifted her weight while checking her watch. "I'll let you know," she answered. I let out a nervous sigh, for it took every ounce of courage to approach her. Sometimes I wondered if she could hear my knees knocking. Yet we got to know each other through secrets that would last a lifetime. I grew older and somewhat bolder and always willing.

On one particular day, she was in a great rush and asked me in. I had crossed the threshold; her musk was passionately intoxicating. I saw the tension in her garter straps pinning her stubborn nylons into place. The straps framed her thick limbs; fine hairs fanned her inner thigh before curling and then caressed her "v". She stood before the mirror with hands on hips. I couldn't stand anymore. I approached in a trance. There was a gleam in her eye when she ordered me to help with her bra snap fasteners. She was tall, but her wide behind was on the line with the head of my dick. I tried leveraging myself so I wouldn't lean. But I stumbled; she moved so that I was resting on her fleshy cheeks with me nestled in her deep crack. It was good. I did all I could to prolong. I strained for an eventual release. My pants grew warm and wet, leaving a stain in the wake. She murmured, then squirmed, arching her hips as I slithered deeper into her crack. "There! Is that better?" she asked, settling more into my lap. It felt so good to snuggle in the heat, feeling her ass cheeks clinch in massaging me into a slick, rumbling fit. I came again! She just smiled, saying, "Come back when you're older."

My dreams played on, complementing the sensuality of this woman's greatest asset. I'll always long to take her into my arms and kiss and nuzzle the hollow of her throat while caressing her breasts. We'll dance to a slow strain. I'll groove in the shadowy crevice; I unhooked her bra. I'll find my way into her bedroom, where I'll fasten my lips to her and send my tongue deep.

The years passed. Her beautiful, thick, dark hair was now streaked with gray. There were no old feelings I had to recapture, for my fascination with her had remained active since the first day we met. The game resumed without much shame. Flashback scenes overwhelmed once more as a boy lost in the fantasy of what I would do with her behind the known locked door. What started long ago had yet to be consummated. The time was now; she stood before me in lust-crazed modesty stripped to her waist clenching corset with arousing garter straps slapping at her full and luscious flanks! My eyes bucked wide as she bent forward, showing the deep, dark crevice! "Would you like a ride?" she said with a bedeviling smile. I stumbled from the chair; my heart skipped. That ass was bare as she arched high. I speared her with lips and tongue! She stopped being smug as she let out a yell. "Why?" she asked but got no reply. I moved into her rump. She didn't know I could make my tongue curl. I teased with a thumb and pushed, skewering her puckered hole. Her eyes grew wide with a sudden awareness that she was about to be had—that she had unleashed a beast and that she was the prey. I hugged her full ass as she bucked to break free. But the strength in my arms wouldn't deny me. Now she was being slashed by a merciless tongue swirling her g- spot and setting her ablaze! Her breath came in sharp gasps; cries of ecstasy filled the room! Shock waves surged the brain! She was losing all control to the tongue licking her hole! "Oh! Why?" she moaned; tears streamed her cheek. Why waste time when it was what he wanted? When was he ever going to stick her? She would fade to black, then if I would ride her, all from the back! I heard her questions and beseeching cries. "Oh no, say it isn't so! I had control! Ride rough, but give it slow." She didn't seem to mind giving up control; she backed and ground into me. I erupted and exploded, draped across her back continuing the plunge in to feast on her thick, quivering rump. She struggled, but I held fast and drained life's essence from her trembling body. We tumbled until I caught one limb, hooking it over my shoulder; her thigh slammed against me; lifting and caressing while guiding me into her. I wallowed in a sweet grind mound-to-mound, exciting friction's blaze.

Her legs splayed wide. I speared her repeatedly; she bathed me in her slick, swirling juices. Orgasms burst in an awkward entanglement of our arms and legs. And after some wine, we shared kisses, fanning the flames. Head down, ass high—we both began to cry. Profound and complete, sweaty and outright nasty—giving more than either could stand. We drifted into sleep; across the painted desert, warrior and steed galloped, gathering strength, making sure the curtains were drawn shut, for what happened next wasn't meant for the eyes of children…

A Divine Intervention

. . . Her muscled limbs secured a bond . . .

Lea Reynolds stripped; her subtlety burst into a generous flow. Her blessing was received by the real connoisseur of full- figured women. However, compliments cut like a double- edged sword; all wasn't well in this holy hamlet vying to hear her confession. Tales abounded; holy men and deacons lured the unsuspecting into the lair for a swift taste of absolution. Lea sang with heartfelt solemnity about how the spider devoured the fly; she was ready to repent for sleeping with the Monsignor.

The Pastor declared it a 'New Day' with determination to bring order to the congregation. The pastor knew the Monsignor's demands went beyond the cloth and beneath the skirt of the most devout. Nevertheless, Sister Lea was more impressed with the majestic power the Monsignor yielded with a smile; wrestling with this man would be like tangling with the devil. However, anything would have been better than submitting to damnation for not accepting the Monsignor's will. The pastor had been cut from the same mold as the Monsignor, just as it had been for Lucifer to Satan. Monsignor's sweet words gathered at the crotch of Lea's well-stuffed panties. He waited for her skirt to rise past her silky-smooth thighs. He was all eyes when those fat legs came into view. However, the Pastor's jealousy came to bear. Obsession devoured Lea, who pounded at the Monsignor's hips. Passion distorted her angelic features with guttural cries and flailing thighs.

The Pastor observed all. He held Lea accountable for dark, musty corridors and his form of penance. He wasn't one to be fooled with. Lea grew anxious and more willing to do what he wished if it meant getting the Pastor's absolution. However, the holy man was slow and deliberate. He looked past tenets calling for mercy as he prepared the sacrament. Lea slipped her panties and straddled the minister seated on the old squeaking bench. He barreled into her like a fist stretching a tight fit. They rocked to a thrashing cadence, grinding, humping, and mound-to-mound. Flailing limbs overturned a lantern. The gates of Hell opened and claimed two souls. Screams assailed the flames, consuming all in its wake.

The alarm clock sounded! My bed sheets were drenched with sweat. The nightmare claimed sleep and continued to torment during the day. I could still hear the voices of two souls crying out; the internal flame consumed. I should have left well enough alone after being run down by a Gypsy cab that humid summer night in the city. I was late for a hot game of Poker, and a chance to win back what I had lost the week before. A victory would never be sweet. I thought to step off the curb and into the street. A bright yellow cab burst from nowhere and came to a screeching halt.

One could still smell the burning rubber. Perhaps I was to blame— or maybe it was no one's fault. I had a ready answer for anyone who thought accidents were humorous. Sandalwood memories played to her swiveling hips.

"I'm all right," I replied, embarrassed at the attention mixed with anxiety, thinking of a game I was sure to miss. Someone was going to pay, but the passenger's full limb clouded all reasons. I ran after her. "Your purse" I called, spotting it at the curb. I stumbled to retrieve it. "You forgot your purse!" I would have snatched the money before returning it. Like I said, someone had to pay but had it not been for her tight-fitting skirt this man might not have been so honest.

"Glad you could make it," she replied. If she didn't have a manager, I was going to apply, though what I knew about the music that amounted to the size of a pea. Business was akin to the size of a pea rattling inside an over-inflated beach ball. "Singing was God's plan," she said. "That's why the gift should be shared," I reminded her.

"I am reaffirming Faith!" I said when my religion remained bounded by a tight-fitting skirt. She went cold and gave a sly smirk. "You have greedy eyes and merciful heavens if you think your posturing will get you some; you're just plain out of luck." I assured her this wasn't a booty call. She was taking credit for turning her first convert. "How much are you willing to commit?" she asked.

"That depends on who and what I'm committing," I said.

"You need to meet our Reverend," she gushed, heightening the stake to sweeter possibilities. Her assumed innocence made the play a little too easy. I wanted to scrap this scam and get out of Dodge. Lea's thick body had blind men talking about seeing again. Damn! The heat and humidity were about to claim another convert!

"You need this more than I do," she said, offering a fan and dabbing my brow. The gesture was something mothers were fond of doing to their children. "It gets warm when you least expect it," she sighed. Not only did it get humid; it gave reason to run. The scowling minister moved toward us with the speed of a shepherd warding off wolves. Still, I couldn't draw my eyes from the lady's stretch across the pew in retrieving a fan. Her luscious reach threatened the fabric of her skirt. The Reverend understood my intentions very well. If anyone were equal to grappling with the Devil, it would have been the imposing Reverend Laws. He wasn't quite so benevolent as he was a shrewd politician who had gathered a loyal following by putting food into their bellies. He kept the lecherous—me—at bay.

The Reverend practiced celibacy with the belief that it released man of carnal bounds in providing spiritual enlightenment. I argued celibacy was not God's law; it was a flawed interpretation by the Church. His handshake confirmed his point of view, setting doubt about him being pleased to meet me.

"I didn't get your full name," the foxy sister reminded me. "That makes us even, I didn't get yours." "Lea," she said.

"Lee Warner," I replied, breaking the Reverend's grasp. He bellowed with laughter. "There is room for a lost soul," he added. I didn't appreciate being referred to as being 'lost'; his humor reminded me of one who enjoyed plucking a fly's wing.

"You wish to reaffirm?" He replied, "What caused this divine intervention?" Sweat sprouted legs and crept down the center of my back like a bug crawling along my spine… "A Gypsy cab!" I said, apologizing to myself for not coming up with a better answer to slap that sneer from his lips…

"Ha!" the Reverend said, gesturing like a fat bird trying to fly. "God's ways are mysterious indeed. The truth will shine this Sunday morning. You may attend if you dare." Whatever he meant; he made it personal.

I reserved Sunday mornings for sleeping off a Saturday night binge— chasing the wild rooster. Competing with the Reverend was the last thing on my mind.

"He's something else!" Lea gushed. I had to admit he was something else. The punch line to this riddle went no further than the femme fatale standing before me. Poppa once said, "Women with glasses aren't innocent as they appear"—that when it came to religion, there was more to her than an eagerness to serve. I knew what I had wanted until I met her.

I chased her through the corridor. "It's not meant for just any man," she said in all the confusion. "Are you ready to commit?" The way her ass was grinding, I was willing to commit to anything. "Sister, stop," I said, answering taunts from the inside of me. "Let me hit that ass."

"Sister Reynolds, do not forget the fundraising benefits this evening," the Reverend called above the dispersing congregation. It sounded more like a command; she was duty-bound to obey.

However, thanks to the Reverend's challenge the dilemma was resolved.

My scheme was clear. "Let's begin tonight," I offered. She added her number with a note that read, "Please call."

I called Lea the next day and the days that followed. I kept getting busy signals and began to think she gave a phone number to get rid of me. I didn't sleep well that night. Visions consumed me, ending with thick scissoring limbs drawing me into her, hot and dripping. It had me racing to the refrigerator and recalling a time when life was much simpler. I was about to hang up, when…

"Hello?" It was her! The number was real!

"I was beginning to think you had changed your mind," she said. "We can start whenever you're ready." Nevertheless, she was proving to be a master at deception, where everything she said seemed to have a double meaning. I got into her past that started in Louisiana.

She had been a finalist in the state's gymnastics competition. Her talent for mathematics earned the scholarship. She dabbled with singing, wrote song lyrics and performed in local clubs that paid her bills between gigs. She modeled lingerie and married the photographer, but reality stripped fascination from romance and led to divorce.

Her nightclub singing resulted in Saint James, where she became a lead soloist and a part-time accountant.

I was ready for religion after perfecting my most devout expression of repentance. I rang the doorbell. And there she stood to offer a striking contrast from the benevolent Sister to the seductive enchantress. Both presentations proposed an exciting aura to match her dark piercing eyes and vibrant red-brown complexion with soft red undertones gracing her sensuous lips. The lights were turned down low—not what I had expected for religious instructions. Excitement danced in her eyes.

Her short tresses cascaded the back of her neck then curled and tickled the corners of her mouth. She wore a cinnamon silk long sleeve blouse with the top button open and a powdery blue scarf. A beige skirt ceased its journey just above the knees. Fat legs filled out black nylons, with feet perched in off-white stilettos. She had returned from a successful singing audition.

"You didn't bring that bottle to just talk about religion," she said, pointing to the brown bag I held. "It's meant to release evil spirits," I replied.

"I am sure it will," Lea added. She knew very well what was on my mind.

"No ring on your finger?" I asked.

"There's no point in bringing up old memories," she replied, chuckling and adding, "Chalk it up as a case of not wanting the same things and finding lipstick stains on his briefs. "I had to move on." She laughed, saying, "Or it would be another night with over-cooked TV dinners." She got back into the dating game, finding most men wanted to get into her panties. "A one-time friend called me by mistake and left his phone off the hook.

As I listened, I realized he was in the middle of fucking some bimbo. It stopped my heart. I started to rub and he went deeper. I came so many times that I fell in love with that moment."

Lea won my sympathy, but the stirring from my loins reminded me that hard dicks had no conscience; toss all protocol to the wind. It was all about me. I just didn't give a damn.

"Now I have shared with you," she inquired, "what are your thoughts? Can you handle me?" she asked, "Tear me up or have I given too much?"

"That doesn't explain why you took your time answering my calls," I said, all the while about to explode! Damn! She had fat legs! She still hadn't released the past and maintained a certain amount of distrust, yet she answered. "You seemed different," she went on to explain. At this point she didn't have to; I grabbed a magazine to hide the stain spreading while remembering old adages about never looking a gift horse in the mouth, and just take the money and run. Lust's pressure had tears beginning to well in my eyes. I was about to burst

She continued, "I liked how you stood up to Laws." I didn't see anything heroic about the flogging I took. It was the first time she saw anyone stand up to him. I asked how she and Laws ever got together in the first place. "The Reverend is a good man," she replied. "That's what attracted me." She mentioned how late humid evenings spent reconciling account ledgers, and an open desk giving a full view got the balls rolling. "I didn't mind his gawking. I was doing a little bit of my own," she said with a gleam, and then added, "When I drew my skirt, his handsome face was glistening with sweat. (Not to mention what she was doing to me right now!) He stood with a bottle of wine and pressed it into his crotch. He appeared like a little boy looking for a place to set that bottle. I mouthed the words without a sound: "Fuck me!" But he didn't get the message; he offered a warmed taste. I accepted. He stumbled into the waste paper basket. His clumsiness won my sympathy, gathering at the crotch of my panties."

"After the wine, some light conversation, and few stolen touches, me and the Reverend didn't complete ledgers that night. He was thick with my cat," she said, just working me into a gushing, slick, sticky, hot and sweaty fit. "That man sure could slam," she said, "but his criticizing the length of my skirt put an end to our 'love.' He wanted to know what was in the note you and I exchanged. I refused to answer. He called the next day saying he needed help with his Mission. It's all good, as long as he understood my mission had nothing to do with his getting into my panties. You know how you men are," she said without a glance. "Trying to get over."

The brown bag reached its mark … It had me wanting to kiss and lick from the crown to the backs of her thighs. She twisted and then pinched my lip. The pain had my eyes rolling. The script had been switched. "I'm sopping wet, ready for some swollen meat! And you're just down there licking?" Short skirts and diaphanous shirts set my testosterone level on a rise. "You did me wrong," I said, playing the game." … "Twist me, make me squeal!" Lea said. "ARE YOU GOING TO TALK ALL NIGHT?"

My hands were inside her D-cups, cradling big tits. "It's getting warm," she said, with friction inching her skirt. Long garter straps burst into gleaming snap fasteners. We kissed, searching for the other's tongue. I gathered her panties in dissecting a fleshy rump. We tumbled. She rolled, breaking my hand. I slipped her panties and caressed her plump rump with soft and deliberate finger strokes. "Don't stop!" she murmured, sweet and weak. The pounding of our limbs entwined overturned a coffee table. Had it been a candle we would have gone up in flames.

Her demands kept coming. I held and lifted her into the crook of her knees and hoisted her limbs over my shoulders, forcing her thick thighs in crushing her breasts that spilled across her chest. She split open in sweet rapture as I plunged into her. The dove cried! Orgasms surged to a deep, tight, slurping grind and then exploded, taking me high to be gathered by her fluttering wings.

What I believed flashed in sensations and her moaning. "Oh baby, don't stop!" I encircled her hips for sanity's sake as she arched in a swayback motion with a tilt of her hip that locked me into her gaping grotto. She snarled and hissed like a beast in heat. Rivulets of our passion erupted as blood rushed, then abandoned us to a thumping bedpost and whining bedsprings. She screamed and bucked, with my nut sack slapping her quivering behind, reduced to a writhing mass of flesh. We swooned to sweet pleasure as I marveled at her rhythm, a well-muscled rump, a repeated stutter like a well-timed jackhammer. Our misty eyes met for just a moment as her fat legs encircled and then rocked me to sleep.

I awakened and burned that old card deck, asking, "What time do Sunday services begin?"

"About the same time, I have you committed," she said, showing me the front door.

"Funny!" I replied. "That's what they said at the asylum." She wasn't laughing. Just then the telephone rang. It was the Reverend. We both were locked in purgatory and fighting our own personal dragons, giving us more in common than I cared to admit. The difference was that he hid his soul in dark garments.

Mine lay bare to the sun. Yet I was far from being anyone's champion. But for now, my purposes were clear— steady the foundation. How things change and at the same time remain the same. This time I had a purpose.

Unrequited: Love

Helen's dark side had warned me before the split lip I got for entering her bedroom without knocking. I saw her big ass- crack, ever so deep! I would be emptying my sack if left alone! "WHAT"! She exclaimed, catching me as I tried to hide, "Trying to bust a nut? No sir, you had better hold up! Just letting my ass air out! Go away! What I got you couldn't handle." However, I sure would like to try. I couldn't ignore her grinding hams encased in transparent black panties. "It's not nice picking up my skirt," she scolded, attending the split lip she inflicted. "Your playfulness will get you into trouble."

Helen never dreamed she would have to mother two, one being the father and the other his son. On this particular evening, Pop called saying he would be late because of a poker game that couldn't wait. Helen had cause for concern when father's friends included those who stayed one step ahead of the law and smiled when they wanted something. She remained concerned when he hadn't returned. I didn't mind because it allowed a riddle concerning a butt plug in a laundry bag with a collection of magazines. If anything, it showed that the owner of this treasured stash proved wise when it included dozens of condoms in all colors and sizes. The butt plug held the greatest fascination. I was tempted to use it on myself just to see how it felt when I flipped the page of a magazine and got stopped by one full-figured woman who bore a striking resemblance to Helen.

Excitement grew with the size of the model's ass, showing how that fleshy rump shadowed the back of her great big thighs. The next scene featured her lying across a huge brass bed with the same butt plug nestled between her massive cheeks. Speculating how it was used aroused my curiosity; I tried it and damn, did it ever hurt! I couldn't understand how anyone could take that knob and smile. However, one thing I did learn was the difference between smiling and grimacing. Graphic photos in the next scene showed a pimpled-face jockey with a lascivious grin. He tugged the woman's panties and inserted the plug between her clapping cheeks. "Is this what you want?" he asked. The lady arched ever so slightly, replying, "Of course, you fool!" The next scene showed the woman's face down on the pillow while the jockey plugged and plunged that handy nub, making the Amazon wider. He then mounted her. "OH! OH!" the woman grimaced. "It hurts!"

I could tell Helen appreciated the attention with my comparing. "You look better than those women in the magazine," I said, watching her test the temperature of the warm bath water. She straightened up, knowing I was standing nearby. "You should leave those books alone," she quipped while gazing at my crotch and adding how a cold shower would be in order.

I lay awake thinking how much I wanted to sink between her thick cheeks. I asked if I could share her bed. She laughed, saying, "I don't think that would be a good idea." I begged to lie next to her. With some thought, she obliged, saying it might be all right. Never one to question a woman's motive, or look a gift horse in the mouth, I took the money and ran. She turned onto her side. The great indentation of the mattress had me flush in her rear, but she was fast asleep. Familiar stirrings returned. I snuggled to smother the ache at the center of my loins. In a dreamy state, Helen turned, saying, "I'm glad you are home, darling. How much money did you lose?" I realized then she was mistaking me for her husband, who would be extending a long thick limb across her thigh, allowing me to slip beneath her to enjoy a sweet grind. I rubbed and pushed as our body heat soared. She braced, taking me with her. I held deeply implanted between her writhing buttocks. Sweet pleasure, overwhelmed. I heard a door slam shut. Father was home! I had to think fast as I stumbled out of his bed, grateful he was drunk.

"Is that how you feel?" she asked with a coolness that belied the heat I felt when I was beneath and grooving her thick rump. I became the fly on the opaque wall in tune to the lust behind the closed door. I saw it all. Father went berserk! "Slow baby," she said while skillfully turning him on to his back and then mounting him. She held him by the throat and initiated a gyrating, swiveling thrust, thoroughly taking control as both rushed to the edge. She raised her rear through sweat and a tear, plunging without mercy. She whimpered; he locked his arms around her waist and surged, giving more than she could stand. Her toes curled, and her hips did the swirl. He tried to get out but remained deep in her! "Hold it," she said through clenched teeth. "Don't make me slap you because I sure will!" Their grunts escaped beyond the closed door and into the room; the loudest growls were of animals in heat as time rushed in a blink of an eye.

The child became a man; inspiring ambition giving way to obsession and visions of a fateful night haunted in the wake of unrequited love. Her distorted image reflected from an old shattered mirror. Ideals and dreams became elusive and teasing through my formative years. My newfound awareness lay in unlocking the door and finding the perfect woman but with caution not to hold too tightly.

Lingerie

I closure to affairs that were doomed from the start. Always looking sipped from an old brandy glass, toasting an all-night binge that gave and never quite finding. What better way to forget? Love had a lot of us singing a 'how my baby done me wrong' song. "Snap out of it!" Bret, a trusted bartender who had a sly way with women replied. "I got this invite!" His eyes lit up to emphasize a crooked grin that crept beneath his well-trimmed mustache. "There's going to be more booty than the law allows." He had made a connection with a receptionist at the A-Plus modeling agency during an emergency service call. "It's an invite to the annual 'Ball' where women strut their stuff and 'D-cups' overflow," he sang. Thick hips swiveled and muscled flanks strained… It had my interest, but just for the moment; as this particular moment was meant for bellying up to the bar. I had other things on my mind, like how to make a move without making it seem too obvious. I took another brandy and contemplated the depth from the surface to the bottom. Bret always had the answer. "Very simple," Bret the barroom philosopher replied, "go along with the flow." And like most philosophers he rarely completed a thought but invited the mystified to complete the thought themselves with consequences should they guess wrong.

So, I went along with the flow. The night was sedate, sophisticated and sweet. But something was wrong with this picture. I expected dance, some conversation, perhaps a little romance from the front seat, only the women smiled and offered their hands to those who didn't seem to care.

Had I done something wrong? Bret hadn't bothered with particulars about this affair. Whatever the theme, I couldn't help feeling I was taking a beating because of it. Solving riddles prompted me to leave. But on this blustery evening where the temperature plummeted to twenty-five below zero, it became wise to stay.

Lights dimmed to the seductive strains. Women chose partners. My ego took another bruising. All eyes seemed trained upon the spot where I stood. "Be cool." Bret advised that at 'Sadie Hawkins' women did the asking. "Play it their way." I caught on; the women did the asking at the Sadie Hawkins Ball. Bret walked off with the secretary. Soon their shadows could be seen writhing to a delicious strain against a cold opaque wall. Yeah, I had finally caught on. Yet it may have been too late, so I got cozy with a shot of brandy and decided to sit this one out.

Before long, a new arrival had entered the pool. There was hope. Her name was Earlene. Built like a fireplug with an asset to take the title, her features became soft in the fading light. Mystery danced in her smile. Men stood patiently for her to choose. The gleam in their eyes reflected my own. It would be a foot race, but we dared not move, for he who did would be leaving alone. And so, I nodded a hello and passed her by.

There was more to her than short cropped hair and a little dab from Grandma's pomade. Broad hips inspired. Heat radiated from thick and well-muscled thighs. She proved raw, raunchy and ready, challenging anyone who thought talking trash would have her willing to give up that ass. One brother replied how he would suck her toes or so the story goes. She slapped him in the mouth, splitting his lip. Some offered to reimburse for every dollar she had ever spent! Her mystique had them strung out all across town. But tonight, they had to stay rooted to the floor, for it was Earlene's option to choose.

The mysterious Earlene had a past bounded by a subtle touch of class. She had come home bedazzled by what she saw. Her husband was socking it to a spindly wench. Earlene screamed. She packed a pistol but rushed into the streets with tears streaming. Her great cheeks clapped. She stepped high, flashing her spell. Lusting hounds begged for her name and number. She had just gotten in from Chicago. One slick talking brother got all beside himself trying to learn the name of the lady. They ended up at her place. He nearly went blind when he saw her. Earlene sipped a brandy mix. Before the finish, they were up against a wall and Brother Jasper was in charge.

Earlene didn't mind all. She remained fascinated by his quick jab. But when the talk grew cheap, his tongue swirled. She swung a riding prod. He yelped but stayed fascinated by Earlene's round eye! She warned him to stay away. But Jasper proved stubborn and more determined, despite the awful riding crop Earlene wielded. She tore up his ass, but still he wouldn't let go! "You know I want that round eye!" he maintained. Earlene grabbed and pinched his ears. That brought the brother to tears! He gave in to Earlene's grin. She kept the whip by her side. Suddenly, he stopped. Earlene felt something pop! He trembled and shook. The brother blew his top. His balls were drained to the very last drop! All he had left was a sheepish grin. "It's your fault for showing that wink. You can drive a man to drink. Earlene ushered him out the front door and slammed it shut. "Tell that to your mama!"

Earlene was in heat and revenge would be sweet. She caught her man riding a trusted friend. The two didn't know Earlene stood nearby. The husband kept on pumping the friend's fat rear. Earlene went home and packed her bags and found an apartment on the Upper West Side. Frustration gnawed as she got ready for the party that she would attend alone. And this is where I came in.

'Sadie Hawkins' was in pursuit. I wanted to appear worldly as I sampled the buffet. She passed the others in asking me to dance. "Don't blow this one," a voice from within warned as I tasted her warmth as her body moved against me. She was as sturdy as a tree stump. "My savior wears a bolero skirt," I said, drawing her laughter. I enjoyed the silky smoothness of her fabric that guided my fingers to the fullness of her luscious rump. Earlene moved gracefully. We shivered and dipped to a grinding stride.

"Mister," she whispered, "where did you learn that fall?"

". . . At the asylum," I replied. I wasn't into small talk. "I'm a nut- loving squirrel." Guests weren't paying much attention to us. They were for their own private pleasure. "You're coming home with me," she said, and then added, "I am going to hurt you real good."

"This I got to see," I said, somewhat amused and a bit cautious as to what I had gotten myself into. I doubted myself—for that moment.

Black tongs bulging at the crotch—moist and dripping. Had I removed her panties then, it would have broken all the rules. But rules were made to be broken! Lights grew dimmer. I was grinding against her ass. Long garter straps cut into her flesh in drawing nylons to the vast expanse of her thighs. Her mincing walk displayed her grinding roast. I grew even more excited imagining how the straps tightened and how her hips swayed beneath her skirt as her fluffy ass shook with each step: I wanted some and didn't know how to make it happen. But as Bret had said—go with the flow! Yet a sudden flush of anxiety set in and had me tossing all caution aside: This was mine. And though that crack about the asylum had frightened most, this diva didn't budge. "A kiss to your momma for giving you booty."

Earlene bristled. "I don't know who you are or where come from, but how do you get off talking about my mother? I see your bug eyes staring at my legs and thighs! You want to laugh it up, I see!"

"There's no need for you to get loud," I said. "That noise will draw the kind of attention we don't need. Besides, Bret will kick my ass if I don't shut up and go with the flow."

"And who the hell is Bret?" Earlene had to know. "You and your boy both need a head check." Bret once told me how he ended up screwing his boss at a bar mitzvah celebration. He did everything to make her laugh so hard that before she knew it, he had her over a bar stool and fucked her. She kept squirming with a slight lean, lifting him off his feet.

"Where's your man?" I asked, expecting a husband or boyfriend to suddenly show up. "He should be punished leaving you alone."

"It's none of your business," she replied. "You bug, my man and I love each other very much, so get your hands out of my panties!" From her outburst, I could tell all wasn't quite right in paradise. "I left him," she added. "I knew how to make him holler and squeal. And I can do it to you if your momma let you stay out late!"

"When was the last time you had a meal?" she asked. "Sounds like an invitation," I replied. Earlene grew bolder as she began to stroke me, saying, "I like what you got. Can you make it jump?"

"I'll answer when I get you alone." Earlene is one thick and curvy lady! I thought in awe. I was determined to just have fun. But it became quite amusing—acting foolish and not caring. It gave me a cover, enabling me to examine her while I remained invisible—not taken seriously for the fear of being hurt. "Hold me back! Is all that honey going to trickle?" I babbled. "Are you going to save me a pinch?" I continued, "I will savor every inch."

"I see you've got a way with words," she said with a chuckle as the music began to play. She took my hand and added, "You're not as shy as I thought." We leaned into each other's arms and enjoyed the dance. Her movement was slow and deliberate. "You're coming home with me," she said, "but make sure your insurance has been paid!"

"Are you that confident?" I asked.

"I'm just sure about you," she replied.

Earlene's bedroom was an intimate enclosure of lace and silk abounding in red. Earlene issued a soft chuckle as she returned in a long, flowing off-white transparent gown. "A little something, I bought for special occasions," she said, eyeing me. Her thighs seemed larger set off in 'V' cut panties, garter belt, and black nylons. "Move slowly!" Earlene said, massaging me. She reached for the stereo. I reached for her. We struggled. She resisted, wrestling from the sofa to the hardwood floor. Slapping and swishing echoed throughout. Earlene accepted sweat and the awful humidity while coaxed into a spread-eagle grind. I stroked and choked and bellowed like a moose. Fantasies and visions took me back to a time when I saw this big leg librarian climbing a ladder. Her billowing skirt bared a devastating flash of her panties straining to hold her. We were both taken by surprise, locked in an awkward position. Somewhat embarrassed, she snapped, "What are you looking at?" My eyes rushed and jumped all up and into that lush rump. And then she smiled, as if realizing that her embarrassment mirrored my own, by asking, "Are you enjoying yourself?" I ran from that library with her laughter echoing from behind the closed door.

Earlene was my second chance to a moment that had haunted me ever since, until a prayer had been answered. I pinched. She squeezed. We wrestled. She cried out, saying I was rude to be rubbing against her. She squirmed as her eyes rolled and fluttered! She twitched, trembled and sighed. We fell onto the bed, where she glanced across her shoulder and arched her rump and held it right there. Earlene backed it up and arched into my lap. "Hurry!" she gushed. "Strip my panties!" Her body heat offered no more pretenses; this was real! I rose to my toes and delved with a pounding, maniacal surge.

Her hips thrusting upward served notice that she was past primed. We continued the grind in the quiet of her room. She led me to her bed. Grandma's pomade permeated with fresh leather. Tight dark curls graced and traveled, forming an inverted triangle. Earlene hooked, and then she fried and cooked! I let my tongue dance about her navel. She moaned when I split her with my tongue. "It's just for fun. I don't want to hear from you when we get done!"

I was mad with lust! She had me with my face between her thighs. Her fresh leather musk fragrance had me thirsting for more. I drew back. She blinked and shivered. Her honey-swamped gash was swollen! There was no need to be talking trash. I had hooked her panties, stretching them across that broad rump. The narrow strip shielded tight curls streaming her inner thighs excited me into fly between her fat legs to smother the ache escaping from my loins. The thick bristle tickled—just right for nesting. "Honey!" she cried, throwing her head back and meeting my grind with a powerful upward roll of her hips. She had me against her slick crotch, all the while cooing like a love sick pigeon. "Just wanted a good look at what you're working with." Her fingers whipped and popped buttons before she engulfed me in her steamy hot mouth. I took hold and stacked pillows beneath the bowl of her cheeks. Within, warm fluids that had built up in her were now overflowing in torrents!

It was then that she looked down the valley between her legs and our eyes met. The sensation mingled with vulnerability, inspiring me to take her. I made my way up her smoldering frame and slowly entered. She arched her neck up and kissed me, her own juices trapped in my mustache and her French manicure getting embedded in my shoulders. I slipped each inch into her; her eyes widened and I had to coax her to relax and take me in. She adjusted as I issued a slow twisting thrust. Earlene could barely speak, but neither could I as we cried into the night with grunting sounds that were meant for birthing babies. We surged mound to mound in a grinding fit. I hoisted her legs over my shoulders as she pleaded with me. I didn't know whether to be flattered or to ease up. But when she mewled and bucked, taking my thrusts and holding fast, the answer was clear. Stretching her increased a maniacal thrust. We surged as I lifted her knees so that they rested against her breasts. She screamed from what I couldn't determine as being passion or pain, but she continued to cry as she held and spanked my flanks with a resounding and clutching slap. I answered like a jackhammer gone berserk. She cried from the depths as her body shivered in convulsive fits. But just as suddenly she lay still and yet contented. Her eyes were gleaming into the distance. I would've given my last dollar to know where she had traveled, but she smiled and asked if I wanted more.

"You're ready to take advantage of me with that tool!" she moaned with a deep guttural but playful sound. Again, I could hear that big leg librarian taunting. The years had drifted in a flash. I was exhausted then, as a youth, because of excitement and now because of drained stamina. I could barely get it up! "Oh no, not me," I answered. And I had little intention of going backdoor when taking flight became a better alternative.

"You're a liar," she moaned. "You want to drive me out of my mind?" What I wanted was a way to bow out gracefully by savoring the moment and maybe come up with a poetic expression of gratitude, but grunts were all I could muster.

Silk ribbons exploded into another jazz soliloquy … Her nylons were in threads. Skyrockets took flight. We cried out with little shame! I speared that tight canal. "DAMN! DAMN!" she screamed, tripping the edge with scissoring limbs.

The Cure

. . . His redemption . . .

The serpent slithered; probing fingers surged. She arched high then plunged. Pleasure echoed in mewling cries; gasping agony and grunts escaped. Dr. Joyce Lamont massaged woman's most sacred treasure. That brown eye winked and barked at the moon. Women cried, shivered and fried. However, the python stood waiting in the shadows. Dr. Joyce Lamont possessed an uncanny resemblance to promises that vanished when the alarm clock summoned. Dr. Lamont was about to make a significant announcement to the National Board of Neurology, an innovative cure for impotency. Cliff Richard, the roving consumer reporter for a small-town newspaper, covered the press conference. Few knew Cliff held a vendetta against the doctor. It involved his wife Flora and an appointment she set with Dr. Lamont to discuss Cliff's marital dysfunction.

Cliff planned a late-night dinner at a newly opened Midtown restaurant to surprise Flora after he appeared at Lamont's unexpectedly. Flora kept the appointment; all was going well. However, women who sought Dr. Lamont's advice were often seen rushing from her office dazed and confused, stockings skewed, and their garter straps undone. But a quiet smile curled the corner of their mouths, teasing imagination as to what went on behind Lamont's closed door. All remained on the down-low.

On the morning of the press conference, Lamont appeared with dignity and purpose, in contrast to how she appeared the night before with Flora, with her limbs raised high then pushed back into her breasts, making her thighs spread wide to take the serpent's glide. The cure for impotency caught the world's attention. No one would have guessed the remedy meant cracking nuts with a strap-on dildo.

Cliff arrived on time, but he was the one surprised. The office lights were turned low; the staff had gone home except for the moans coming from the adjoining room. Dancing shadows: Flora and Lamont? Thoughts rushed like electricity spiking one's tongue after being caught in a back draft to a raging fire. Betrayal whispered with the crush of the women tumbling onto a heavily upholstered sofa. Life had a way of evening out; nevertheless, spying had a price that Cliff bore for his indiscretion, spying upon women who played in the shadows. His punishment was just beginning. He wouldn't have been held responsible had he a pistol and pulled the trigger. Instead, Cliff left as a broken man, haunted by what he had seen. Flora didn't return home until well after 4 AM. Pride and ego took a beating. Cliff became the intruder who suffered the women's scorn, grinding and plunging to the python's girth. He could still hear whimpers as the python split to the depths. Lust-crazed torrents and desire merged with unbridled passion. Spasms erupted in a copious flow; a cramming session had Cliff bursting and finally spewing his seed.

Dr. Lamont was beginning her practice when Cliff's wife Flora sought guidance in coping with an impotent husband. Lamont remained unaware how much she affected the young writer and his quest for an interview. Lamont didn't owe him anything, but perhaps she did. He had written articles featuring women in a profession man typically dominated. Lamont's career soared. Cliff remained grounded until he landed a position with a local newspaper. An interview with the renowned Dr. Lamont would help his career. He dreamed of submitting to her healing. However, Lamont had little time for an unknown journalist. He wanted her head down, ass high. He would jump that booty and lock himself to it. She bucked like a mad bull.

Cliff went tumbling to the floor. "Ready for more?" she teased, arching a little higher. It was all a dream.

Cliff woke up drenched in sweat, a cruel reminder of what he had witnessed: Flora and Lamont slithered with fat thighs grinding. Thrashing! Squirting! Gushing juices flowed. The show was not heaven-sent! It became a brutal reminder that he would never enjoy the lush flavors of his sweet Flora!

Cliff couldn't get it up! Flora sought advice, all the while thinking she was the problem; that her husband had lost interest in her. She grew suspicious, accusing him of cheating with their thick butt neighbor down the hall! Too many times she caught him eyeing that big behind. Nevertheless, Cliff remained unaware the woman was more interested in Flora. All seemed fair and unapproachable until that hussy returned his smile. Flora flew into a rage. She needed someone to tell her what to do. This play led to visits with Dr. Lamont, whose treatment required a double-headed dildo.

Discovery came to a head when Cliff met with Flora that night out on the town, hoping it would help in recharging their marriage—at least for that evening. He arrived, finding the doctor's office shrouded in darkness.

Everyone went home; he heard whimpering cries and saw Flora teetering at the edge of Lamont's leather couch in a grunting frenzy as Lamont's head disappeared beneath Flora's skirt.

Lamont held a huge rubber duck! Despite her passion, Flora could barely control her laughter. "What do you aim to do?"

"Put a hurting on you!" Lamont said. She massaged and stroked until Flora trembled. She moved to avoid, but Lamont was quicker with a strap-on dildo. Flora clawed the cushions while the doctor humped. Flora glowed from the ravaging blows. She stood on weak knees and in a daze all but collapsed. "I ought to bitch slap you!"

Lamont said, wiping her lips and looking on with a smirk. "Don't make me put a hurting on you!" "My turn," Flora replied.

"Who gave you permission?" Lamont shot back. They tumbled to the floor where Lamont's thighs smothered Flora, working her way between thick legs. Flora returned home until well after four that morning. Cliff pretended to be asleep; however, pride and ego took a beating. He was the intruder. Lost visions repeated Flora upward thrust to a plunging python's slithering surge. It left her cruelly distended. Cliff could still hear their whimper in lust-crazed torrents playing to a cramming session that had Cliff spewing his seed.

Cliff returned to being flaccid and weak, as if lifting weights with no hands. Visions assailed a fevered brain. It festered like an open wound, hastening a quick retreat. The other woman, who turned out to be his wife Flora sighed and cried to Lamont's tongue. She thrashed in a passion like Cliff had never seen.

The Neurological Psychiatric convention came to order. Critics argued that female neurologists were seeking thrills. Whatever she preached, Cliff wasn't listening. Nor was he listening the night he rode her ass into the shadows. Keeping their distance would have been wise. Neither could blame for appearing at the convention. It all happened by chance that Cliff covered the story. He watched with eyes locked to Dr. Joyce Lamont's grinding rump. Small feet perched in stilettos gave a delightful arch to a thick ass. Her classical features teased in an off-white gabardine suit as a white satin Nehru Blouse gleamed under the lights. Corn rows set to a beehive hairdo added to her mystique. Brown eyes turned in deciding a catchy phrase.

Cliff, the reporter, noted how he would make her eyes turn as he settled into her. Obsession dictated his resolve. Harsh and cruel, he wouldn't be satisfied until settling an old account with Lamont.

There was the truth in Lamont's well-documented quest to cure men's suffering. However, Lamont's methods were of concern among the profession. Still, wives and girlfriends seemed usually pleased with the results. For Cliff, it became a personal crusade to expose Lamont's practice and have her license revoked. Lamont treated the wife's anxieties but destroyed an already-doomed marriage. Lamont's action became the straw that broke this camel's back. Cliff sought to destroy Lamont but found himself trapped with needs of his own. There lay the key to carrying out the plan! Did Cliff present himself as a patient needing help?

The receptionist quizzed him on the method of payment. "Cash or credit card would be preferred," she said. It appeared that Lamont's caring equated to the size of her client's bank account. Cliff complied after some haggling and was told to wait in an adjoining room until called.

Lamont's pinstripe jacket and matching skirt completed her professional appeal. Cliff prepared for their private conversation but couldn't draw his eyes from her feet perched on stiletto heels. "Recordings are not permitted," she said. He turned the recorder off but tripped the switch to the super-micro unit hidden in the crotch of his briefs. Lamont warned her treatment was progressive in comparison to other neurologists, and that if he felt offended, he could leave and his money would be refunded with no questions asked.

Damn! He was good looking, Lamont thought. She hadn't felt such an arousal since her early years when a blind date stood in for her boyfriend who had stood her up for the school dance but then too late had a change of heart. Lamont slipped away into the backseat of a 57 Chevy. She couldn't ignore the stranger's sweet words and his hard body pushing against her. Her reluctant boyfriend arrived to see her eyes roll in answer to the strangers thrust. "This was not for you," she moaned. "You're lying," the stranger replied with laughter that rang and haunted for years. "You wanted it as much as I did!"

Lamont returned to her studies determined not to be easy for just any man. However, something about Cliff brought back memories Lamont tried to forget. "Have we met somewhere?" she asked. "Maybe a telephone conversation?" She was getting warm.

Cliff and Lamont rushed toward a head-on collision. Lamont lowered the lights, ordering Cliff to undress. He placed the recorder and slipped into a clinical gown. Lamont pulled the pin holding her beehive. Braided tresses cascaded to her shoulders. She removed her eyeglasses and disappeared into a small dressing room. She returned in a diaphanous black corset made of the finest Belgian lace. Ribbons woven into the garter straps drew nylon tops and framed broad hips. Sheer panties cupped thick hairs fanning from her navel and teased her inner thigh. Flesh bulged at the border of her bra cups. Tightly drawn stockings squeezed the meat of her fat legs, causing them to rush her thick limbs.

Long armpit-length kid gloves were so tight on her meaty arms that she could barely move her fingers. Wondrous assortments of curves held in check by exciting undergarments gave the impression that if she sneezed, the room would explode with bits of nylon and lace. A smile curled the corners of the doctor's mouth. Her eyes caressed Cliff's shoulders and tight butt. "You better remove your trousers. Don't mind me. I have five brothers."

What that had to do with the tea in China? Cliff thought.

Cliff unhooked his belt and dropped his trousers. Lamont's low- slung D-cups jiggled. Big tits bulged with excitement. Nipples protruded through the fabric. Already thumb-size, they seemed to swell even larger.

"Are you embarrassed?" Lamont stammered, mindful of the doubt that had hounded most men when they were standing naked. "Don't be silly," Lamont protested. "What would be the point in soiling your trousers? And this way would be more comfortable," she casually added.

"If it doesn't bother you, it won't bother me," Cliff answered, working his briefs along his thighs. Lamont grasped the back of a chair and wasn't behaving professionally. Her breathing came in sharp, quick pants. Black enchanting kid gloves graced her upper arms. Gloved fingers worked vigorously in massaging him. She shivered with fever, sending her curves into violent motion. Pendulous melons flopped about her ribcage. Fleshy hips quivered down to her thighs, billowing over the tops of her nipped in black hose.

Lamont took him. They sighed and stumbled. She caressed him with a gloved hand; her trembling fingertips brought warmth. Frustration mounted. He would have sold his soul for a firm erection. Relax and enjoy the heat, she said, once more betraying professional tenets concerning overblown protocols between doctor and patient.

"No need to rush," she said with the confidence that had been his. Self-doubt continued with a flush, but this time it tickled, sending electric sensations carousing from the back of his neck and along his spine and centered at his groins. His nerve centers were alive—that was happening now.

She stretched across an upholstered leather gurney. Again, Cliff marveled at the high rising slope of her ass and how garter straps cut into the well fleshed behind. She ordered him to strip her remaining garments, but to leave her stockings intact.

Cliff rolled Lamont's panties and stepped with him poised to strike. The expanse of her thighs appeared to spill over the edge of the gurney. He bathed her lush body with warm oil. The massage eased thoughts about all Lamont had sacrificed for the sake of professionalism. Cliff escaped flashbacks to an estranged wife.

Muscles bulged in sheer black nylons. "Call me Joyce," she said, abandoning formality. No one referred to her as Joyce. Cliff had crossed an important threshold. Her oiled nakedness glistened. Lamont guided him into her dark, inviting crevice.

She moved her lush buttocks into his lap. Cliff gritted his teeth and cradled her breasts while working her nipples between his forefingers. He nuzzled her throat while flushing her ears with hot breath. He plunged, sending her limbs pounding at his hips.

Joyce shivered at his tip pushing into her and triggering orgasms as she ground into the leather gurney. Cliff mounted that gurney. Joyce Lamont contracted about him and held him fast. Cliff savored the sweet snug fit as retribution juices flowed. Lamont collapsed with him draped across her quivering hunches. "Oh! Oh! Oh!" the professional drooled. Cliff reentered her gaping portal as she secured him to delirium that rained in the throes of passion.

Screams assailed in gushing torrents. She wanted him in her ass. Lamont bucked and swayed, accepting his girth. The lady's stamina reduced him to a shivering mass with each twist. She siphoned the last drop. "Push baby, push," the thick woman said, gazing through lust clouded eyes. Doubts Cliff held with his being of stature continued to haunt him; however, passion had a way of quieting his demons.

Joyce propelled her luscious buttocks into him. Thick thighs flashed, and garter straps strained. "Just keep it in the oven. We'll bake the chicken in gravy until it's sweet and tender. Rest awhile and I'll give you all the interviews you can stand," the satiated therapist said, adding, "You are ready to go."

When Cliff got back to his apartment, he gave Flora a call. Why wasn't she answering? Perhaps a late-night shopping spree? He didn't know Flora had returned to the doctor's office, intending to forgo all protocol and find her place between the Amazon's large, shapely thighs. Voluptuous bodies thundered, and limbs flailed: Flora had gained the advantage, with Lamont on her back as sweaty legs clashed, obscuring the snake to a ferocious grinding. The women gasped, writhed and squirmed in unison. Flora's betrayal ceased at redemption abounding in her husband. It placed sweetness in getting even.

Absolution reflected denial that became hatred but gave way to forgiveness. Cliff returned to Lamont but hadn't bothered with knocking as he entered. Flora knew it was her husband; lust stole his ability to speak. She could tell from his musk and sweat. He stripped; she arched high to engulf him. Cliff grasped his wife and surged into her shivering rump like a hot knife slicing through butter. Lamont rocked beneath their pressure, forcing her limbs to stretch wider for the python to finish its tease. Sphincter spasms sputtered and jumped! Flora forgave her husband who was housed deeply within her, busting nuts and riding that butt as tears streaked her cheeks. He drew the curtains, for what they were doing next wasn't meant for the eyes of children.

Let Me Tell You about Rita-Mae Johnson

. . . A surge into a seething inferno . . .

Rita-Mae Johnson kept men off balance as they sought to impress with the size of their hammer, a real tight jammer that would seal the deal. Rita-Mae smiled and men were aroused, but in this flame with no real shame women longed to sample her charm. How insecure and depraved all became when thinking of Rita, when all she wanted was respect. Most declared that their quiet need was about her anatomy and wondered at the pleasure it would bring. No one bothered about offering a ring. Nevertheless, the suspicious found cause to worry when their mate disappeared at Rita's gate at any given hour, as they have done many times before with simply a knock at her front door.

Rita wanted more, and relying on women didn't satisfy her curiosity; it heightened interest in a sudden change in lifestyle. It gnawed at her conscience, leaving sorrow and a trust that betrayed her. She wasn't about to share a second date with either sex. Still, she learned 'never to say never'; then came Minister Lee with eyes toward the sky. He sought to soothe her with a lullaby. Minister Lee spent the night, much to her delight.

Passion soared. He held back with all his might, trapped by Rita's need hovering in shadows of the distant moonlight.

So complicated was the union with Minister Lee, who was into saving souls. He had to be tested against celibacy-like doctrines, a flawed interpretation of religious tenets. Minister Lee prayed to the Lord to sheath his sword. "Please don't test me. . . Not down there where she touched me," he implored.

Why hesitate? Why wait? It's all about hate. Rita's seduction quaked in taunting his manhood that very day. All the while Minister Lee refused exile as he struggled with conscience and an unholy smile. All he could see was her voluptuous full-figure in settling the score. His obsession grew; he didn't know what to do. Quick as a blind bat he did fly, with a generous dab of nature's KY thrusting and humping and not caring why. He stuffed her gaping, quivering brown eye. Stumbling and mumbling, he plunged, incited by Rita's sweet cry: "Minister Lee what are you doing to me?" He was packing that oven with a whole lot of shoving. "That bread will keep me well fed," she said with no reason to measure; just enjoying that treasure giving her pleasure. Let it rip humble desire, leaving Minister Lee in liquid fire. It seared the humid sky a rooftop scenario became a lullaby. Satan's faithless Jezebel had taken over Rita's soul, thrusting and grinding, making the Reverend feel it was heaven-sent. And before very long with much intent, Minister Lee was more than willing to pay her rent.

Minister Lee in hiding his concubine, an isolated convent he did find. He buried his sword but soon Rita got bored hearing him cry for his Lord. He assailed the heavens for what he had done. It brought pain as a tribute to his blunder. Without protest, Rita grew tired and packed her bags and headed west. Finding divinity became a holy quest and a solemn test at a College of Divinity that would suit her best.

Surrounded by mountains of the great Northwest she caused a calamity. Gyrating and swiveling kept the faculty aware. Rita could toss a salad while balancing the bowl on her rump, they were told. She had her way, a sweet soap fragrance mixed with musk, betraying trust and getting attention from far too many. Illusions had men rushing to soft conclusions gushing from the dark, releasing pressure before final exams. They imagined her arching high enough to make a grown man cry. Take a rip into her sass just riding that ass. Oh, how she did sigh with wide-open brown eyes and a smile that drove men wild.

Then there was Angie, Rita's lover, whose body produced thunder and gratitude at Minister Lee's blunder. It set Rita wandering. When she met Angie, it set both aflame; no one was to blame. Their booty caused toilet seat noise because men were lost in private wonder playing with their toys. Angie showed style with internal grace. They took to the dance floor, not meaning to hurt with a flirt; the uninvited was going to get hurt. Riding the rumble taking a tumble with their eyes fixed as they surveyed, but then they settled on each other. They both knew how the game was played though it meant committing to Hell. Increasing vexation without hesitation spurred the need, inspiring greed into an invitation to a celestial rendezvous just meant for two.

Rita and Angie moved in together. The desire was to punish by Teasing without pleasing man without much dread. Angie and Rita tumbled into bed the night after grinding across the floor. Hunger burst; they did dine grasping in a perfect 69. Buried in thick hulking thighs, excitement exploded from their brown eyes. Tongs went darting at the prize, quivering and delivering; it was all so fine, like vintage wine. "Who wants to talk?" the roommates said after being well fed, ready to taste those nipples until an explosion. Strip those panties and get into bed—foolish words; straddling thighs will bring tears and dark circles beneath lust-clouded eyes, echoing the early sunrise and recalling the day they toured a clothing boutique trying on sheer panties and walking the floor. They put on quite a show, shaking that booty, getting into the flow. With a start Rita let it go. A two-way mirror drawing nearer let all see including a brother hoping to gain some recognition. He talked so much trash his jockstrap holster came undone. His tool burst into view. Brown eyes cried oh me, oh my!

They got out fast with a taste of brandy that got patrons stoned out of their mind and longing for that broad behind. Rita took off in full flight into the night. Men spun in disbelief at the sight. They chased through the door, fat legs moving quite fast—how long could it last? Chasing without relent, all sexed up with the vicious intent, offering to pay every dollar she spent. To her dismay, they wouldn't go away; bound and determined to run her down, taken with fever and searching for some reliever, they were like a hound covering the distance across the ground. Soon they began to fall away in dismay. Rita had gotten away, which haunts the pursuers to this very day. Many went to an early grave with regret for what they could not get.

Since that day, Rita met this writer at a dance, giving him a chance for a little romance. Rita seemed eager to accommodate. Someone would get lucky. Rita could lift her partner off his feet with a rolling motion, hot and sweet, shocking all in the house; not a creature was stirring, not even a mouse. She decided to sit but couldn't quit, her skirt rising high to large rounded knees. "It's not to get cool, it's just to please," she said.

I kept my distance let the saga unfold as players competed words of wit. She passed them by. I've seen her do this before. I headed for the door, walking past her. She acknowledged my presence, but I kept walking, yet cursing the gamble I was sure to lose. My arrogance, pride, and ego were about to doom me with regret. And yet I wasn't about to grovel at her feet. I moved on, but Rita took my hand as if I was her man.

I went along on a dare. I accepted the dance, enjoying her dexterity that had me in a trance. She swayed and pranced, throbbing with the rhythm beating in my chest. She had been watching me from the corner of her eye, wondering what my next move would be. Rita was my height; with red stilettos she towered over me. I was searching for something to say; she laughed, kicking her shoes out of the way. Magic strains began to play crotch to crotch no thoughts of leaving. Her belly, heaving arms entwined like a clinging vine. My hands came to rest on her broad behind. Rise! Assail! My pistol had just been fired. I lay in the wake, clutching walls, aching balls speaking in tongues couldn't take it anymore.

Rita's grind, her thick behind—it was a risk, shame with blame. Who was going to end this mating game? Losing control trying to be cute, playing a game in trivial pursuit; standing in the cold pretending to be bold. I would have been the next story told. Words were lame; I'll take the blame. Stroke her thunder; let her eyes widen in wonder. I just didn't care! "Don't stop my dear, you're doing fine," Rita crooned as if reading my mind, clutching my behind. We danced across the floor. I fixed a plan; selling it was going to be ugly.

"What can I do to ease your pain?" she asked smilingly, tilting her head and turning her lips toward mine. "If it's all the same," I casually said, "lay your head on my bed. Like your skirt until the morning with panties on until the Dawn. I'll keep your condoms nearer just in the case for a ride instead of a frivolous chase." It was easy to see she agreed with me.

Time won't go to waste; skirt down tightly about her waist. The music faded. I walked away, feeling her eyes on my back, relieved that I hadn't gotten slapped; a calculated risk, I turned and left. It was rude I must admit, but it made me high because of it. Time drifted; the dance came to an end when someone tapped me on the shoulder. It was RitaMae in all her glory begging me to continue my story.

Rita cut to the chase, still amused well into the game without much shame. "My roomie won't be around," she said. "Angie is out of town; my panties are down," she added in haste with her tight skirt hiked high across her thigh. What was in that punch, I wondered? She whispered my name, "Shane. I think it's sweet that you want my booty; time for you to do your duty." Echoing the words I heard again, I played along with a grin that bordered on disbelief.

"What can I do to ease your pain?" she asked. Clouds grew darker; it began to rain. "I want you," I finally said. "What's stopping you?" she replied.

I sought to save her integrity, taking it slow, not letting her lover know.

How I'd be riding and not letting go, causing her lover to go insane and I end up with a bullet in the brain. I marveled at her high rising arching rump. She stripped, leaving her panties on for me to rip. Her lover must never know.

Rita teased with serenity as she arched high, increasing the pleasure, impossible to measure, keeping rhythm, arching still higher as I did fly. Her massive spheres tossed and bobbled against a crystal doorknob, arching her back with her panties intact. I became the mindless jockey, humping that thundering rump. I continued to rock, rubbing and stroking from side to side, friction burning to a rustic sleigh ride as panties slithered at her ankles. She engulfed me with intensity.

Weeping, vision blurred, I couldn't see. Spasms ripped from the hip. "Oh Shane! Oh Shane!" she said, spreading her thighs, welling tears in her brown eyes. I continued to move in her panty groove, reaching the spot of her bulging crotch; blazing a trail, she began to wail: got to believe me, can't you see? You got to go; if she found out it would hurt her more than you will ever know.

Rita's murmuring, "Oh you make me want you. I can't let you go when you're under my skin; I'm losing my mind when you're in my behind. Take me again where the sun doesn't shine." She was losing her mind and I wasn't far behind. Our final encounter wouldn't be by chance. Her rage grew and then it flew, troubled by what she was about to do; re-wrestled to the floor. "Don't you say no more." Visions dance inside my head. "You're in trouble now," she said with a scowl.

Judge nor jury will find me wrong; why was she singing this fearful song? "I'll tear your ass. You got no class," she said, jumping and bursting a seam. It's going to get nasty and quite damn mean. She punched and kicked. I took a grip, grappling at her flaring hip, and then I slipped. She just grinned. "I'll tear it up good like you knew I would." "You just might but not without a fight," I said, keeping my dignity well in sight.

"You want more?" she said from the bed. I was dead like my good friend Fred. I thought it better to get up and run, a screw was loose and shaking that caboose. Rita wasn't dealing from a full deck; my body and soul she was about to wreck. Spread that button, just having fun; continuing with sass to shaking that ass—isn't that what you want to say to have it your way? The door was locked. She didn't stop; my eyes were about to pop. Her muscular tail continued to wail. We rumbled and tumbled across the hard floor, slamming against the damned closed door. "You ripped my panties!" she said accusingly, and yet she was still playing me.

"You knew darn well riding this booty meant condemning to hell." I began to grow weak with her haunches seated on my chest, pounding the breath out of me quite effortlessly. She was bent on smothering with her hairy nest; wouldn't let me rest before tasting her crest. "You have yet to pay; you have yet to play. I'll haunt you now both night and day." She wrenched me, sending white hot flashes exploding behind my eyelids. She held tight; I lost sight, but heaving with all my might propelled Satan's daughter on her back. I began to attack.

"Shane," she said with her right leg hooked over my shoulder. She kicked in a violent storm. I slithered her crotch; her gasp-gaping gash into her ass I did thrash, smoldering words of wit and all that trash gurgling and bubbling to a tight smoke fit. We surged, rising to the hilt. She began to milk, riding side by side. It was quite a ride. "Let it rip," she moaned and sighed. "Oh, Shane do it to me!" Giving love; rocking her cradle beneath the stars above.

She opened wide, grabbing her ankles and pulling back. The bells did chime one at a time. I was in that ham like a white-hot knife, slicing that spam. Not a word did she utter that meant for me to stop. She arched high. I massaged that eye with a touch of KY, nursing the length in a tight snug fit. She swayed and dilated, saying it was heaven- sent. Contractions hit.

Our bodies were in sync, floating at an obscene angle. Minister Lee became a memory. "Don't spare the rod; give it to me hard," Rita beseeched, calling my name simply as Shane. All that sass just riding that ass; her massive rump like a runaway sump pump, grisly absolution. Lost in the scriptures we grunted and groaned, baking the chicken with a thrust beginning to quicken. The fever mounted as I encountered each spastic twitch to scratch that itch. I wanted her bad, driving me mad.

"Just lie on your belly across my bed; keep your panties." Rita's eyes glowed with the question concerning discretion.

"Is this what you want? You are blowing our secret," she said. The feel of her fleshy rump ready for another soulful home grinding and finding her hand had slipped beneath her hip; supporting the bowls of her ass within my grip. Nut sack knocking against her, a heartfelt gasp popping a gleaming garter belt clasp. I split her panties and spread her wide then slammed once more. We tumbled to the floor, settling the score. The finish was never so near. She groaned, "You nasty bastard! You have no will; take me, my darling, do what you feel. Grab my ass and make it real." All was intact. Fat cheeks slapped and then engulfed. The earth beneath me began to tilt. She blew my mind.

We wrestled to the floor one more time and then we heard a pounding at the door. It was the Minister and Angie with broken hearts. Their listening to the sounds behind the locked door fueled the fire, lusting dreams with infernal desire. It drove them mad remembering what they once had. In one active voice they did entreat that if we didn't open up it won't be sweet. They were going to break it down, right down to the ground. Toilet seats thundered clear across town. No one was getting any sleep. I was in pretty deep. Sultry cries—she began to weep; giving it to me we weren't about to sleep.

I must say it was time for the Minister to pay for his blunder. Teasing his hunger, continuing to rise, mounting fury across the old wood floor, merging shadows did consume passion rumbling through the room and had the Minister wondering at silhouettes creeping across the wall, leaving him standing in the hall.

Stiletto Heels

. . . Her Coke-bottle figure fed a most passionate appeal

A...searching. I was willing to beg, borrow or steal like an addict freelance writer is only as good as his last assignment and asking for a fix releasing me from a severe case of writer's block. I kept coming up empty until a glossy centerfold featuring a full-figured woman lying across a large brass bed. A smile tickled the corners of her mouth as her dark, piercing eyes followed me across the room. I took another swig of Granddaddy's liquor, inflamed with obsession, desire, passion. However, it left me searching for something with more than just a bit, something more than another pornographic tryst between the sheets with inspiration settling as a tease.

Somewhere and somehow in this great city, I was going to find a story. But my being trapped like a deer in headlights standing on a crowded subway platform with the thundering approach of the streaking Manhattan-Bound wasn't where I hoped to find it. I cursed the conductor, who thought teetering on the edge was humorous. I claimed the last seat and swiftly dozed, only to be awakened by the marching sound of stilettos. A tall red kinky-haired woman in a tight- fitting red gabardine skirt appeared. I found my story, but she wouldn't look my way, seeming more interested in a marked graffiti poster. Her honey brown complexion took me. The elegant white satin blouse teased her narrow waist, complementing full breasts coaxing her nipples to pierce the delicate fabric.

It was just a guess, but I was willing to bet that this flower thrived in the Crown Heights, a section off Flatbush Avenue where flyaway red wooly hair with the other side waiting for long corn rows was fashionable.

It didn't take a philosopher to realize this sister was accustomed to deep knee bends. In short, her presence was intimidating. A passenger nudged another and exclaimed to look at that caboose! He dropped a few coins, giving cause for him to stoop for a better view. Told everybody he knew, that ass is hairy for sure! Some laughed; women glared and appeared threatening, as if I had orchestrated this scenario. A more sympathetic female quipped about how she would never have dressed like that before the rush hour. Strangers smirked, adding sympathy couldn't feel that sack of potatoes. Men wouldn't quit suggesting strapping her with a saddle would be ideal. Yet a scorching glance from Miss Stiletto said it would be a bumpy ride for the uninvited.

My story continued to flow though Miss Stiletto wouldn't let on what she thought as she stood aloof with eyes fixed upon a graffiti collage poster. Her weight training guru lectured how strenuous routines transformed the fatty tissue into muscle but failed to inform how muscle fiber hardened inches she was trying to lose. Beauty was a matter of one's own perception.

Were we friends in another life? Perhaps classmates in a setting where she attempted to fit into to her surroundings; she just wanted to belong though scorned by others. It must have broken her heart when the boys laughed, saying how she looked better in the dark. She would raise her hand, but never got her chance as the teacher would pass her by. My eyes would fill with tears, and inside my heart would burn. Yes, we've met before. I often carried her books and took all the stares and dirty looks. Yet deep in my heart I knew that someday boys would give all they learned in school to be somewhere in the dark with her. Insecurity bred their intimidation. It cast a tall shadow; the kids didn't know how to approach her.

She glanced in a mirror but was disappointed at the reflection she could not hide with dieting and hours of aerobics. This lead bucket, she thought, would sink a battleship; so unaware that the ageless masters had honored her with timeless portraits and sculpture. I pictured her returning to her guru, who answered with inspirational clichés. However, such clichés left her with one solution: Stay away from the pool, particularly when she couldn't swim. Perhaps that's it, she thought after being left with little recourse, flaunt it! Perhaps that's why she stood aloof: homely girl, she was so lonely. Now she's a beautiful woman. Yes, that ugly girl, that lonely girl; but she hadn't forgotten the boy who sat beside her. The one who'd like to hold that place his whole life through; she was beautiful to him.

Her presence complimented a Coke-bottle physique. The train rumbled, jerked and screeched to a stop. The sudden shift knocked her off balance, leaving her reaching frantically for leverage that drew more attention to flexing loins with dignity teetering on stiletto heels. I gaped like the rest but offered my seat that an elderly woman quickly claimed. "I would have given it to her anyway," the voluptuous Stiletto replied. I continued with small talk, finding she was from my old neighborhood. Once strangers and now friends. More passengers boarded to the sudden engine lurch, pitching me against her.

Apologies didn't help; she arched, bracing my fall, and held me fast. The engine started, throttled and jumped. Each vibration had me sinking deeper into her grinding rump. I once cursed this subway system, but now I was blessing it. I braced for a backhand slap. Instead, she replied with a barely audible whisper just to hold on to her hip and that she wouldn't let me slip. All the way into Wall Street terminal and without much warning, we surged into the quivering station.

The seductress waved goodbye, stepping into the crowd. I rushed after her and got trapped in the tidal wave that swept me into a waiting elevator. "Hello again," a familiar voice responded. I had backed into her. I pretended to be relaxed and casual but dripping sweat gave me away. "Stalking is against the law," she said. "What makes you think I'm stalking?" "A stiff intuition," she replied, now playing to the crowd whose eyes were trained on me. Suddenly the elevator jammed with my butt resting in her lap. "Now it's my turn," she replied. I apologized once more but succeeded in losing a witless battle and reminding her how flirting with strangers could be dangerous.

"Didn't your mother teach you anything?" I asked. "Now you are insulting my mother?" she countered. "What do men call you?"

"Bitch!" she said with a wink. "What do your faithful companions call you?"

"FOOLISH!" would have been a better answer had the elevator doors not opened and saved me from further embarrassment. She disappeared into the rush but left a card. All that remained was her lingering sandalwood fragrance and that card she slipped into my pocket that read *Veronica James*.

She worked for a Wall Street accounting firm. I couldn't resist her invitation. We met that evening for dinner. All went well until she mentioned the Manhattan-Bound and the stalled elevator. Sweet possibilities sparked a verbal joust that included insults right through dinner. She had me reeling like a man who suddenly caught himself in his zipper. Yet I couldn't deny being aroused by this lusty woman whose whispering nylons inspired bedtime fantasies.

We finally reached her apartment. "Are you inviting me in?" I asked. Veronica didn't bother with answers, but left but door ajar. She rushed to place the kettle on the stove. She reached the oven; her mood became ever so slow and most deliberate. She retrieved a dish from the lowest rung. *How inviting*, I thought. She held her pose. I'm the winner, the lucky one. Veronica seemed to be reading my mind and smiling seductively. Those early morning hecklers may speculate about the depth of Veronica's thick behind on her belly and arching across the brass bed.

Veronica showed little pity for the timid, who would be sobbing had they known what adventures this writer was about to encounter for respecting a father's advice to his son concerning the social norms concerning women. My mind was in overdrive. I took particular notice of her great grinding rump and fat legs complemented by crisscrossed calf-high sandal straps.

Veronica proved fascinating as a three-dimensional drawing of a cube, indeed. The more I found about her, the more she left to be uncovered. "Yeah, I bet you would like it sopping wet," she said with a cruel grin. "Just getting to know you conversation," Veronica laughed, reveling in her vanity and saying, "If you want me to get down, tell me so." She had me on the run, but courage resurfaced in a bottle of dinner wine consumed earlier, prompting me to step forward, raising her skirt and encircling her waist. "It's about time," she said, shifting awkwardly and straddling my knee.

Veronica's transformation was complete. We stumbled over a coffee table. Her thighs thrashed at my waist; a muscled limb across my waist nearly broke my back drawing me into her. "The pot's boiling," she moaned, rushing for the kitchen; the phone was ringing. "Don't answer," I said.

"He knows I'm home," Veronica declared, rearranging a tightly drawn skirt, obscenely puckered at the waist. "You'll have to leave," she insisted but turned to me with eyes ablaze, advancing like a cat following the flight of a canary. She discarded her garments, except for her inspiring black panties. Tight curls graced her thigh. Garters came undone with a resounding snap! "We need to act fast," she said, reaching, "but if you think I'm too forward then you better leave and never come back." She guided my hands to her quivering haunches and steered toward the kitchen sink. I had her leaning backward and over the sink, then surged into her with a need that erupted into volleys of thunder. Frantically I readjusted my clothing as she drew her panties to encase her massive hips and great behind while hastily ushering me through the back window to her fire escape. Dominoes claimed her innocence that proved to be everything but quiet as the Manhattan-Bound.

She phoned, knowing I would be waiting. "Come over for some home cooking," she said. I toyed with what her invitation concealed.

I passed up a greasy burger, knowing I was about to be well fed. Upon arriving, I realized this lady had a real intention of feeding this city boy and that the greasy burger I had passed up would not be in vain. The table was set with a heaping bowl of salad. I chased it with an excellent mellow wine, all the while looking toward the kitchen for a steaming casserole dish of smothered pork chops, or a steak garnished with onions. The meal I had expected was not to be. "Red meat with enough fat to clog a bilge pump could hurt you," she said, answering the growl escaping my stomach. This taught me another lesson; When a woman offers a meal, be sure she isn't on a diet. Or sneak a greasy burger before arriving.

We eventually got around to the mysterious call. "It was my ex. He wants to get back with me after I caught him in the bathroom with his pants down." "You should've knocked," I said.

"What? And disturb that brazen hussy on her knees searching for a contact lens that got caught in his zipper?" Veronica replied.

I wasn't about to throw stones. Nevertheless, I wasn't able to reach her, nor did she answer my calls. I couldn't shake feeling her ex was on the scene. It became another weekday morning aboard the Manhattan Bound. I was catching a few winks when I got a kick from someone who had not bothered with apologies. It was none other than Veronica, accompanied by a woman whose proportions included six feet in height and a narrow waist with hips reminding me of a standing bass fiddle.

"Shame on him!" Veronica said, nudging her friend. "Men are such dogs. You'd think the boyfriend would at least say hello. Instead, he's eyeing my girl's booty!" I felt trapped and couldn't deny checking her friend's thick rump. Yet I did offer my seat. But as before, an elderly woman claimed it. Again, I was riding, only this time it was Veronica's British Caribbean friend with Veronica in my lap. "This is so much of a coincidence, even for someone like you," Veronica said, insinuating I had planned this move.

Veronica introduced Michelle and warned me to restrain myself. "Michelle is an accountant with the Internal Revenue Service and a professional wrestler."

Things got tighter; the train lurched forward, pitching me into Michelle. "Easy darling, don't hurt yourself," she said, arching her great rear. "I appreciate the concern," I answered, "but aren't we being just a bit obvious?" She replied that it was all a joke and that I should loosen up and enjoy it. The train stalled and the lights went out. Michelle rocked me into Veronica's lap.

"Can I play?" Michelle whispered, inching her fingers along my thigh. It was a ride I wouldn't forget.

"See you tonight if you are not busy," Veronica invited. "We need to settle an argument." She didn't wait for an answer. I was amazed at how calm the two seemed. They drifted into the crowd. How a man could get work done with those two near was anybody's guess. I called that evening but no one answered. The second called proved fruitful. Veronica replied with urgency. "Hurry, I need you now!"

The lights were low when I arrived. Mats were placed on the living room floor, warming the room into a gymnasium. I had expected leotards. Instead, Veronica appeared in a tight spandex knee-length skirt with her massive grinding rump testing the elastic fiber. She fell into me, almost diverting attention from what I wasn't quite sure, but whatever it was, Michelle was a part of it.

"I missed you," Veronica sighed.

"How much?"

"Too much?" she replied. "Prove it!"

"But we've got company," she said. "Send her home!"

"Hello, lovers," Michelle greeted. I waved a halfhearted greeting, hoping she would take the hint. She didn't. Veronica and Michelle had been teaching an old-fashioned wrestling maneuver, the full-nelson. "Michelle thinks she and I would make a great wrestling team." That settled it; I had to get rid of her.

Dinner was lettuce and tomatoes garnished with cheddar. Then Michelle produced a bottle of Jamaican Brandy. After a few swigs, I settled into the deep a posted Clover. Michelle sat, opposite affording a view of her large rounded knees and a devilish skirt that ended high across her well-muscled thighs.

I was now convinced that having Michelle around might be a good idea.

"We want you to settle an argument." Veronica began to explain her thesis. "Athletes with the largest butt have the greatest driving force. Michelle thinks her lead bucket is superior. What do you think?"

Michelle rose to demonstrate her thunderous behind. I would've stumbled had I been standing. I could measure the size, but how would a rocket scientist test the driving force? I needed an answer. "Loosen up," Veronica said, "you'll find a way." She had faith in me. I took another swig of the fiery blend that had me wondering why anyone would drink this poison without a chaser.

Inspiration: "Raise your skirts!" The women giggled. Michelle was the first to agree and now Veronica couldn't back down. "If that's the way, it is the way it is," Veronica barked. "Then call it the way you see it." Dignity became an illusion. The women walked toward the center of the floor, removing garments and an audacious display of booty enclosed by diaphanous thong panties. Michelle wore black. Veronica proved equally devastating in white. They knelt at the foot of the sofa and assumed the position for a no–holds-barred arm-wrestling challenge. The action had gotten the better of me. I inched closer to sample the musk. I ground into the deep groove of Michelle's thick behind. "Oops, I'm sorry; slipped," I apologized. The touch was hot and wet, slick. It was good. She parted her thighs, allowing a more profound surge. I home grooved, reveling in her heat. But this was their song. The women left the bedroom.

The rumble beyond the closed door echoed throughout the apartment. It became anyone's guess which combatant had taken the advantage. I entered the room. Panties were in shreds and dangling from a slightly skewed lampshade to fat quivering buttocks. Michelle had strapped the black dildo against her and plunged, forcing Veronica to allow the intruder to slither home. The women swooned to rivulets of sweat. I mounted Michelle's massive behind. Veronica propelled Michelle into my gliding thrust. She burst to set the storm's fury, with Michelle draped across my back and body, basked in the warmth of a copious flow.

Afterward a much-satiated Veronica with a sigh denied diet. "Remind me to order a half dozen chocolate éclairs in the morning," I said. That morning we boarded the Manhattan-bound 'A' train. Passengers gasped at the women all aglow. They sauntered to the lustful tune of stiletto heels. Men made comments; some snickered. One stood out from the rest. His ignorance bothered me and I was about to tell him so, but Veronica and Michelle also laughed. "Should I teach him respect?" "You would have us arrested for disturbing the peace, or for taking advantage of the mentally challenged."

Nevertheless, the morning passed. Veronica teamed with Michelle and headed West, competing in the Vegas wrestling circuit. Veronica found time to pass the Las Vegas bar exam. The women pooled their resources and opened a firm managing financial matters for female athletes. Veronica calls whenever she's in town. She wants me to head up her public relations division. We can discuss this over dinner. "Make sure your insurance has been paid," she said. I didn't ask, but I wolfed down two greasy burgers in case a salad dish was the main course. The evening was set, and I was thankful for those burgers. I wrenched my back after a night of serious negotiating, but the job was mine. And as I had once said, freelance writers were always looking for new material and weren't particular where they found it. Whether this venture proves successful, only time will tell.

There's a lot more to be said about full figured women gracing the pages of world literature. An artist preserves the image on canvas and in stone. Regardless of what medium chosen, her place had been assured in the annals of time. It all gave credence to the old adage about beauty being in the eye of the beholder. The last chapter has yet to be written.

~~~~~~~~~
~~~~~~~~~

Printed in the USA
CPSIA information can be obtained
at www.ICGtesting.com
LVHW090748270324
775599LV00001B/189